Sinful Vow

Mafia Misfits Book One

Asia Monique

Copyright © 2022 by Asia Monique

All rights reserved. This book is a work of fiction. Names, characters, places, and incidents either are the product of the author's imagination or are used fictitiously and are not to be construed as real. Any resemblance to actual persons, living or dead, business establishments, events, or locales, is entirely coincidental. No portion of this book may be used or reproduced in any manner whatsoever without the writer's permission except in the case of brief quotations embodied in critical articles and reviews.

Synopsis

Lucia Moretti

I always knew marriage for me would never be to a man of my choosing. As a young girl, I was all too aware of the power I wielded in a world where men were supposed to be the superior gender.

To the underworld, I was *just* a mafia princess. To my family, I was an equal. To my soon-to-be husband? Well, that was yet to be determined. But I pray Enzo Bianchi was ready for me because I was damn sure prepared for him.

Enzo Bianchi

The life I'd seen for myself was no longer an option. My entire world had been turned upside down by the very people who were supposed to be family—my *Famiglia*.

Us Bianchi men were starting anew—forging alliances with criminal organizations who understood our plight. The plan had been simple. Cut and dry.

That was until Lucia Moretti showed up with a plan of her own—one I couldn't say no to. Now everything was at stake, including my heart.

Trigger Warnings

This story includes depictions of violence and talks of sex trafficking off-page; may be sensitive for some readers.

Quote

Sometimes the bad can be good too.

Prologue

The Delegation

al·li·ance
a union or association formed for mutual benefit, especially between countries or organizations.

Six months ago.

Five families were coming together to solidify a unique alliance that'll shake the underworld on its foundation and will continue to do so for years to come.

Dmitri Ivanov entered the warehouse first.

He was a hulk of a man standing at six foot ten, with smooth sienna skin and dark eyes that held deep family secrets he would never share with anyone but his wife—the love of his life, Sasha.

The Russian mafia's Pakhan removed his weapons—a knife and Glock—from his person and stuck them into the box sitting near the door. With the one personal guard, he was allowed to keep with him, Dmitri took a seat at the conference table that held four more empty chairs.

"Of course, we're first," Dmitri's guard cursed in their native tongue.

If Dmitri Ivanov knew how to do one thing, it was how to patiently bide his time.

He'd done that exact thing within his family ranks. Obeying the rules and inner workings of the Bratva until it was his time. What he had to face started long before he was born and at the beginning of his parents' forbidden relationship. After his mother had gotten pregnant with him, by a Black man no less, the terror he knew for far too long started at the hands of his grandfather—a man who had an *old* way of thinking during his time above ground—and later his uncle.

It had been Dmitri's father who taught him what leading a criminal empire consisted of. Along with the sacrifices he would have to make and more importantly, the doubt from his people about his ability to lead simply because his skin was darker than theirs.

Even at a young age, Dmitri knew he was meant to lead his family, but his father, the fierce man who raised him, made that conclusion clearer.

"Patience is key, Son."

He'd taken his father's words to heart and plotted and planned until the right time to strike presented itself. All while working his way up from the lowest-ranking man on the totem pole and building the trust of the people he planned to lead.

Two years ago, rumblings of his uncle's shady dealings and the family feeling betrayed had been all he needed to make his final play.

Dmitri was swiftly voted in as the next Pakhan less than twenty-four hours after having his uncle assassinated. Now that he had gotten the family businesses, illegal and legal, under control, he was taking the advice of his second-in-command

and father and securing alliances with families who had unmistakable similarities to his own story.

"Be cool," he replied after a while, leaning back in his seat. "Patience is key."

Darragh O'Sullivan coolly made his presence known next.

The Irish Mob's boss followed Dmitri's initial steps and dropped his weapons into the box upon arrival before taking a seat across from Dmitri—his guard at his back.

"Dmitri," he greeted.

"O'Sullivan," Dmitri returned, tone dry.

Darragh—being what people liked to call overly laid back—smiled. He found Dmitri's stoic demeanor to be funny. Getting under his skin when they were in one another's presence was the highlight of each encounter he had with the man.

"Still on a last name basis," he taunted with a smile on his lightly tinted face. "What can I do to win you over, big guy?"

"Nothing with a name like *Darragh*."

As Dmitri had known, that made the Black Irishman's attitude change from teasing to dark in a millisecond. Growing up, Darragh was teased for being half Black with a very Irish name that coincidently meant *black oak*. He'd been told daily that he just wasn't "*Irish enough.*"

His mother—a beautiful, no-nonsense Black woman—made sure he had the guidance of her brothers to understand the part of him she'd contributed to.

Darragh felt accepted by her side, he knew what he would face as a man with African roots, but he wanted to connect with his Irish side too. Being accepted by one and not the other built-up resentment inside of him that he still held on to till this day.

His mother took another route, not knowing how to take away her son's pain of not feeling close enough to the man he loved the most. She'd had about enough when a young Darragh came home with his face stained in tears one day. She'd told her son that the next time someone told him he wasn't *enough* to beat whatever their definition of the word was out of them. When he asked what to do with it after he was done, she simply said, *keep it for yourself.*

Darragh had done exactly what his mother told him to do that very next day, decking the first boy to speak ill of his name in the face and continuing to do so until he knew everyone around him would never try again.

His father—Darragh Senior—was a proud Irishman who had fallen for a woman his grandparents took years to accept. But he hadn't cared because if he was going to take over for his father one day, he wanted a woman he could trust with his life and heart by his side. Darragh Senior married the love of his life and encouraged his son to do the same as he got older.

He did exactly that, marrying a Black woman and having four sons with her—who also had to deal with not being *enough* of one and more of the other. The difference was that Darragh had the teachings of his mother and father, along with the help of his wife and her family, to bring his sons up, knowing that they were more than enough.

While they hadn't connected with their Irish roots as they had their Black side, the five O'Sullivan boys—now adults—had joined the ranks of the Irish Mob when their time came.

Darragh was ready to give his sons an entire city to themselves to run how they saw fit, but first, he had to play nice with the likes of an Ivanov.

"If I didn't find you amusing, Ivanov, I'd probably have killed you by now," he said, smiling from ear to ear like the deranged man he was inside.

"Make my day, Sully boy."

The nickname only made Darragh's smile widen.

"I knew you loved me," he mused just as another person joined the meeting.

Mio Sāto whistled her way into the fold. The Yakuza Oyabon—*family boss*—had a dislike for guns and an obsession with knives. Mio chuckled to herself as she tossed six blades—all different shapes and sizes into the box.

"Still bringing knives to a gunfight, Sāto," Darragh deadpanned.

Mio slid her petite frame into a chair before responding.

"Had no clue this was a fight."

She shrugged.

"Wouldn't matter," her husband and sometimes guard spoke up. "What she doesn't carry, I do."

Mio and Joaquin shared a brief silent exchange, her way of showing appreciation for his protective nature.

Joaquin knew his wife was deadlier than the two men sharing the room. He'd learned first-hand just how dangerous she could be after being hired to kill her by her father. The man had gone to lengths to keep his betrayal under the radar by contracting the kill through a Society known for breeding only the most elite group of assassins.

Mio's father hadn't accounted for his daughter being smarter and more resourceful than him. After finding out about his betrayal and the contract against her life, she stuck her favorite knife into his neck.

Mio then set out to find the man or woman who'd accepted the job. Her only goal had been to inform them that with her father dead, their contract was now null and void. Who she'd gone looking for came climbing through her window that same night, making himself known on purpose.

An entire month before that, Joaquin himself had realized why the Oyabon wanted his daughter dead. She was the product of an affair with a Black woman who passed during childbirth. To save face, he took care of her from a distance while she was raised by her mother's family—who happened to have deep connections with Jamaican gangs.

He and his wife never had any children of their own. That made Mio his heir, and the Oyabon couldn't have that. A woman as the boss of the Yakuza had been unheard of, but a woman who was a bastard could never hold that position.

Joaquin covered her tracks after finding the Oyabon dead in the middle of the night, along with two guards. Then, he went to her, and she sliced his face by strategically throwing a knife at him.

"That was a warning shot," she'd said. *"The next one will hit the mark."*

He smirked at her tenacity and then boldly took another step, earning the scar he still wore on his chest almost twenty years later—one that he wore proudly.

To him, it was a reminder of the day he'd fallen in love with Mio and found purpose outside of the Society. For her, it signified the moment she realized her true calling, the one her father had almost taken from her. That was now behind them and today was a new day.

"Well, look who it is," Mio purred at their next guest.

Angelo Bianchi—the head of the Bianchi Crime Family—sauntered into the room without a guard. He bypassed the weapons box and took a seat.

This was Angelo's first meeting with the Delegation.

"Good evening," he spoke politely.

"No weapons?" Dmitri questioned, his thick eyebrow raised.

Angelo shrugged.

"Don't need them."

They were meeting in Angelo's territory, which happened to be a mid-point between theirs. He knew if things went south and he was killed, none of his *allies* would make it out of New Jersey alive. Angelo had a bigger chip on his shoulder than his underworld counterparts. Coming unarmed was a risk he was willing to take.

Leonardo Moretti—the reason they were all there and the head of the Moretti Crime Family—entered shortly after. He removed a single Glock from his person and handed it to his guard, who stashed it with everyone else's weapons.

"Shall we begin?" he asked, taking his place at the head of the table.

He was met with a series of head nods, and the meeting began. Each family had their main business, the thing that made them the most money.

The Ivanovs were deep into the smuggling game, while the O'Sullivans had their hand in the gun trade and drug trafficking.

"My docks are yours," Darragh said before anyone could speak, his gaze set on Dmitri. "You need an entry point for your goods, and we need a new gun distributor. The last one..." he waved his hand dismissively. "Took a bullet to the head."

Dmitri inclined his head in response.

"We would like to host at your casino," Mio proposed, her eyes on Angelo. "One big game a month with all the high rollers Grayfall has to offer."

Mio Sāto and her family made their biggest profits from their illegal gambling ring, while the Bianchi family were loan sharks who owned two thriving legitimate casinos.

Angelo nodded.

"We can work out the details with my son at a later date."

All five parties agreed to share resources that can and will benefit them all somehow. Each of them established territories that were deemed off-limits to others.

"Now that we have territories set; let's talk skin trade," Dmitri said, meeting each person's eyes individually.

Human trafficking was a lucrative business that only a certain kind of criminal organization partook in.

"Not happening," Mio seethed, sending a death glare his way.

He ignored her scathing look.

"May I finish?"

He waited patiently for her to respond, and when she nodded, Dmitri continued to speak his peace.

"As I was saying..." he glanced around the room. "I'm proposing a ban on any involuntary skin trade operations. We know how it works in our world. While I prefer to mind my own business affairs, aligning myself and family with another who use unwilling participants for their own personal gain is against everything I believe in."

"A Russian with morals," Darragh mused. "I agree," he went on, not giving Dmitri time to reply to his smart remark. "Skin trade is out amongst these ranks."

"Anyone against what's being proposed?" Leonardo asked.

No one opposed, and he moved the meeting along.

"Anything else we need to discuss that can't wait?"

Angelo—who hadn't spoken much—leaned forward, his dark eyes pinned on Leonardo.

"I have a proposition for you," he said.

Leonardo lifted an eyebrow.

While everyone else sat quietly, each was intrigued and leaned in.

"As you all know, my family and I recently removed ourselves from the Italian mafia ranks..." he sat back—a thoughtful guise on his face. "Though it wasn't planned, I think you understand why it was necessary."

One by one, they acknowledged understanding his plight.

"Which is why you were invited into this," Leonardo pointed out. "What more can I offer outside of an alliance this large?"

He waved his hand around for emphasis.

"This is promising, but after my experience with my *family*, and I use that word lightly these days, I need a bigger incentive. Something that will keep this alliance intact for years to come."

Leonardo and Angelo stared at each other, knowing exactly where the conversation was heading.

After a few silent moments, Leonardo laughed.

The sound was boisterous and from deep in his gut. He truly found Angelo's proposition funny.

"Are you offering your daughter up for marriage?" Mio asked, her disgust evident.

"No," he replied. "I'm offering my son."

Leonardo leaned forward, his interest piqued.

"Which son?"

"My heir, of course."

"What makes you think my daughter is available for such a union?"

"I *don't* know." Angelo shrugged. "Is she?"

Leonardo took a brief moment before replying. Agreeing to marry off his daughter without consulting her first didn't sit right with him. They had an open line of communication, something he prided himself on keeping intact. But Lucia Moretti wasn't like any other daughter of a mafioso, and the truth in that made him smile.

"If an alliance through marriage is what you need to solidify your place here, then so be it," he agreed.

Angelo nodded and asked, "Anyone opposed to this?"

"Do as you please," Mio spoke up for the group, mainly

herself. "But don't any of you get ideas about my daughter. She is off-limits."

"Such a shame," Darragh said, tapping the table. "One of my sons might be the Blasian beauty's soulmate."

"My knife would look pretty in your neck."

"Sounds like the start to a beautiful union to me," he teased, riling Mio up.

Angelo stood and silenced the table, prompting Leonardo to do the same. They met halfway and stood face to face.

"We can work out the details later," Angelo said, holding his hand out. "In the meantime, a handshake should suffice in front of our *friends*."

Leonardo chuckled and took the man's hand, gripping it tight.

"You have no idea what you're getting your son into."

Chapter 1

Lucia Moretti

No matter how long it took me, I would kill Pietro Costa.

The consequences of my actions would be ominous. Knowing the weight of what I'd set my mind to couldn't and wouldn't stop me from seeing this task through.

I moved up the fire escape of an abandoned building that I'd scouted for three months before deciding it was the perfect spot to make my first move. It was in a dead zone, sitting directly between the haves and have-nots—a line keeping two worlds separate. There were no cameras, no streetlights to give me away, and my escape plan was foolproof if I were somehow made.

I checked my watch, noting the time and calculating how much of it I had before my first mandatory check-in would be required.

Forty Minutes.

Grabbing my one-lensed scope, I cropped low enough behind the building's ledge not to be seen and peered down at the street. The bottom-ranked men in the Costa family worked these blocks—street soldiers whose lives didn't matter to men with titles like Pietro.

They were a means to an end, but you couldn't expect less from the head of a mafia family. I wouldn't put anything past the lot of them, including my own father, who I loved dearly.

The mafia wasn't about love—it was all business.

I checked my watch just in time.

A black town car pulled to a stop outside the secret sex club—*Menage*—two doors down. The driver—who also doubled as security—exited and scanned the area thoroughly. After one more look around, he rounded the front of the car and pulled open the passenger door on the right side.

Lowering my scope, I reattached it to my M24 sniper rifle and lifted it.

Just as I expected, Pietro's heir and namesake was today's visitor. He had a family—a wife and three school-aged children but spent multiple nights in his family's sex club.

The Costa men were arrogant.

I'd only met one up close and personal before, but you could read a man based on his actions—how he moved and treated other people. Pietro Junior thought he was untouchable because of who his father was and tended to linger longer than necessary on street corners that protected him because of his last name.

Too bad he hadn't foreseen me.

His driver moved to the side, engrossing in a deep conversation with the man—more than likely planning his return—and I took my shot, hitting Pietro once in the shoulder. He went down, and I started counting to twenty, breaking down my gun in three and off the roof in five.

By the time I'd reached ten, I was a block away. When I hit twenty, I was behind the wheel of my beat-up Honda CRV, putting my atrocious—yet satisfying—act behind me.

He would survive.

The goal hadn't been to kill but to send the family scrambling, looking for the mystery shooter who had the balls to take a shot at the heir to one of the five thrones in the Italian-American mafia. Business wouldn't flow as smoothly, and that's exactly what I needed to make my next move.

Once across New York state lines, I turned on my burner phone and dialed the only number inside. It rang one time, and then a deep voice picked up.

"Who am I speaking to?"

"Lima-Mike-Seven-Two-Four," I spoke in code, glancing in my rearview.

"Hold," he said, returning moments later. "You're needed in Blackthorne."

I frowned at the mention of the place I laid my head whenever I wasn't working—where my family resided.

"Why?"

Silence filled the line, and I clenched my jaw, knowing I wouldn't get a straight answer.

"You're to report to your father. He will fill you in on why you're needed. Check in when you arrive."

The line went dead, and I shut the burner off, stuffing the small device between my thighs. I drove in silence, watching the road and my surroundings while mentally ticking off reasons I would be reporting to my father in the middle of a job.

I already had a lot on my plate—taking on sanctioned contracts while working behind the scenes on my own. I'd been away from home for over a month now. While I missed my family, what I was doing was for the greater good—the well-being of our family name and its longevity.

Halfway to Blackthorne, I stopped and tossed the burner into the Atlantic. Then, I drove to the storage unit owned by my family in Philly and switched out cars, parking my rusty beater and trading it for my Range Rover.

I checked for bugs and any tracking devices that could've been planted while I was away before grabbing my duffle bag from the trunk where my cell phone was. I cut on the sleek iPhone and slipped into the driver's seat, starting the truck up and sitting back.

The messages started to roll in almost immediately, most of them from my mother—who worried about me the most while I was away—and my cousin Gaia.

After sending out a few messages, I pulled out of my storage unit and toward home, where my condo resided. Blackthorne was a somewhat small sleepy town in Pennsylvania that toed the line of being affluent and crime-filled—my family at the head of the latter. My mother and father had settled there before they'd ever thought about having kids, establishing roots and connections that ran deep.

It was home—the only place in the world I felt the most comfortable.

My safe space.

Inside my condo, I flipped on the lights and glanced around, ensuring everything was as I'd left it. Checking the security system would have to wait for another day.

Satisfied that nothing had been disturbed, I kicked off my combat boots at the door and took two stairs at a time to the top floor. I sauntered into my bedroom, stripping from my black cargo pants, and black long-sleeved bodysuit, and went into the connected bathroom—cutting on the shower to its hottest setting and letting the steam fill the large, enclosed space.

My phone vibrated just as I was about to step in, and I picked it up, eyeing the text from my father.

Two hours, Lucia.

A niggling feeling I didn't like wormed its way into my gut

as I replied back and then stepped into the shower, allowing the multiple shower heads to work the kinks out of my body.

I hated not being prepared, but I didn't have a choice in the matter—not when it came to the people I answered to or my father. So, I readied myself, preparing for the worst but hoping for the best.

* * *

The longer I thought about being summoned by my father and the roundabout way he'd decided to do it, the more it grated at my last nerve—the only one I had left, quite frankly.

I slowed my truck just outside of the gates of my parent's estate. The guards waiting for my arrival immediately began to scan it for any devices I might have missed during my own inspection. I rolled my window down halfway, allowing my face to be seen. It didn't matter that my car was known; the safety of everyone on the other side of those wrought iron bars was more important.

"Welcome home, Ms. Moretti," the head of security greeted, nodding. "You're clear to proceed."

I returned his nod and shifted my truck into drive.

"Thank you, Anthony."

After the guards moved to stand with him, I released the brake and pulled through the gate and up the lit driveway. Once it opened, I took a left and circled to the front of the twenty-five thousand square foot mansion that I'd grown up in.

More guards were stationed near the multiple luxury cars in the drive, some of them making rounds. In contrast, others stayed in place and scanned the area around them. I opened my door and stepped out; the sound of my six-inch heels hitting the cobblestone beneath it echoed.

"Ms. Moretti, do you need me to take your things inside?"

Antonio—Anthony's second-in-command and younger brother—asked as he approached.

Shaking my head, I pulled my Glock from the slot under my steering wheel and attached it to the holster tucked into my high-waisted jeans.

"I have all I need," I said, smirking in his direction.

His lips twitched, but other than that—the too-serious man—never broke character. In his hands, he gripped a semi-automatic weapon—a Smith & Wesson M&P15, to be exact. I eyed the matte black machinery, noting all the differences from the one I owned.

"Is that new?"

He nodded and walked me to the entrance.

"Something your brother acquired while you were away."

"Mmm," I hummed, walking through the already-open double doors. "Thank you."

As if she sensed my presence, my mother appeared, her greedy gaze taking me in from head to toe. It was the same song and dance with this woman every time I returned home.

Nera Moretti was not only my best friend, but the best mother a girl could ask for. We looked a lot alike, from our willowy limbs, mahogany skin, and dark eyes. Her dark curls with red highlights were pinned into a bun at the nape of her neck, while my coils hung freely around my face and neck. And although my mother was more my twin in the looks department than my own brother—who was indeed my twin—that was where our similarities ended.

"Jesus, Lucia," she said, rushing over to hug me and slap my arm. "Learn how to call your mother when you're going to be away for months at a time."

I smiled at the worry dancing in her dark brown irises. She had every reason to fear my long disappearing acts, but I would never tell her that.

"I'm sorry, mama. You know I can't do that sometimes, and this was one of those times."

She rolled her eyes and looped her left arm through my right.

"Why am I here?" I asked, hoping she'd give me something to go on.

There were only a handful of reasons my father would call on me in the way he had. My annoyance, while warranted, was only a quarter of the feelings swirling through my belly.

"You'll have to talk to your father and brother," was all she offered.

The rest of our walk down the long corridor toward my father's study felt daunting—like the beginning of the end. Of what? I had no clue.

We reached the closed door with a guard I didn't recognize and one I did standing outside of it. My mother kissed my cheek and silently took her leave. I watched her disappear and then entered the room making myself known.

The talking stopped immediately, and six sets of menacing eyes turned in my direction. Three sets relaxed after taking note that *I* was the meeting crasher. At the same time, the other three continued to stare in my direction as if I were the enemy in my own territory.

It was obvious by their similar features that the three men were related. If I had to guess, I'd go with a father and his sons —more accurately *made men* with ties to the underworld, same as my family. They were dressed in dark suits, black on black from head to toe. I mentally counted how many weapons each could store on their person and fought to keep a smile off my face. The excitement of being surrounded by dangerous men made my heart thump in anticipation of a fight I knew would never come.

The one standing in the middle perused me from head to

toe. Never one to shy away from being assessed by a man, I waited for him to finish. Eventually, his emotionless yet soulful brown eyes lifted and met mine, giving me my cue to address the room.

"Well, hello, boys," I greeted, sauntering further into the expansive space. "Am I interrupting?"

My father—Leonardo Moretti—stood from behind his desk and rounded it, his broad frame coming to a stop in front of me.

"Lucia," he greeted, leaning down to kiss both of my cheeks. "You're already late. Behave," he murmured low enough for only me to hear.

"Of course."

I'd agreed, but it burned me up inside to do so.

Behave?

Lucia Moretti did what she wanted, *always*, but defying my father in front of his guests wasn't on my list of life goals. As the head of our family, but more importantly, my father, I respected him immensely.

"Lucia, this is Angelo Bianchi," my father introduced after retaking his seat. "Beside him are his sons Enzo and Matteo Bianchi."

Mmm. Bianchi men, huh?

I'd heard stories about Angelo growing up. He was adopted into an Italian family, though he was one hundred percent a Black man. Their reasoning was unknown, but I had my thoughts on the matter.

I spared a glance in my brother, Luca, and his right hand, Dante's direction—both wore impassive expressions on their faces. It was standard for meetings of this caliber to be as unreadable as possible to outsiders. For a moment, I almost broke character, but out of respect for another prominent Mafia family being present, I turned to greet them.

"Pleasure to meet you," I said, meeting their gazes individually.

Each offered a small nod of acknowledgment, and I looked away—forcing back the agitation growing deep in my belly. My body was reacting to something my mind hadn't figured out.

"What's going on?" I asked, staring into the eyes of the only man I answered to at the moment.

"You should sit, Lucia," my brother said, finally deciding to speak.

I waved him off, my annoyance beginning to boil over into my body language.

"Take your brother's advice," our father posed as a suggestion that was anything but.

Once again, not wanting to stir the pot, I took a seat in one of the two empty chairs. I crossed my legs at the ankle and lifted an eyebrow at my father—who, for a brief moment, looked to be apologetic.

"You're needed."

I caught my sigh before it could escape.

His choice of words felt like a stab to the gut. Without needing a deeper explanation, I knew what he meant—where this little meeting was going now. At my big age of twenty-eight, I was being married off to strengthen our family ties.

I knew this day would come eventually.

My father had given me a choice to opt out of being propositioned for marriage ten years ago on my eighteenth birthday. He didn't believe in using women as pawns for family gain, but even as a young girl, I knew the power I wielded—especially when it came to being the only woman in this family who could assist in strengthening it by marriage. More so when we came from where we did— when we were fighting for a place in a society that didn't accept *our* kind—Afro-Italians.

Why fight for a place where you aren't wanted when you can create your own?

There were people who believed we didn't exist all over the world—that we weren't real somehow. We had family just across state lines that would never see us as one of them—they'd cast my father and grandmother out for her family's lies about their origin. DNA had a way of sneaking up on you when you least expected it—my father being the perfect example of that. His beautiful deep umber skin exposed the truth and changed the course of his life before he could form a full sentence.

Nevertheless, he prevailed, putting everything on the line to rise above their ignorant way of thinking. Now I had to do the same. I was somewhat honored to do this for my family. Still, I was annoyed that it would derail everything else I had going on.

I shifted in my chair.

"Which one?" I asked, slowly turning to find those brown eyes belonging to Enzo peering into mine as if he owned the right to do so already.

"Must be you," I said, standing and closing the distance between us.

He lifted an eyebrow and tipped his head, never once opening his mouth to speak. I wanted to hear his voice—needed to know if it was deep or raspy, maybe both.

I knew nothing of this man and hadn't even taken the time to absorb his *very a*ppealing appearance. I did know that my father would never agree to an arranged marriage on my behalf with a man who wouldn't protect me with his life.

Did he know I could protect myself and him if it came down to it?

My lips curved at the thought of that.

"Do you know how to use that?" he asked suddenly, nodding his head toward the gun on my hip.

Mmm. Deep and raspy.

It matched his dark energy, and I liked it.

"Try taking it and see," I challenged, earning a snort from his brother.

Enzo didn't react, nor did he take me up on my offer. That saddened and excited me at the same time. A man who couldn't be baited was a man who deserved veneration, but that also meant he would be no fun.

"I'll take that as a no." I turned to Angelo, his father. "How are the women in your family treated?"

"Lucia—"

"With the utmost respect," he replied, angling his large frame in my direction. "Not only that, but you'll be the Queen of this family one day."

I chuckled and twisted to regard my soon-to-be husband once more.

He was beautiful in a manly kind of way; confidence oozed from his pores. Having confidence meant nothing in this world, but what you could do with it? That meant everything.

Taking a good look at him, I noticed his eyes were a variety of different browns mixed together—being darker in some areas than others. His well-groomed beard smelled of fresh cedarwood and something else I couldn't quite place. The man's lips were thick and had a shine to them that could only be seen from where I stood.

"I don't place value on titles," I said, meeting his gaze dead on. "My self-worth is *worth* more than any title; treating me with respect is enough."

Enzo and I stared at one another, neither looking away until the clearing of my father's throat interrupted whatever was transpiring. I reluctantly turned and returned to my seat.

"You'll marry in a week," Angelo said.

I met my father's gaze instead of addressing Angelo. "Why so soon?"

"At the request of Enzo," was his explanation.

It wasn't enough for me, but I knew he wouldn't elaborate on the details.

"And then?"

My father was well aware that marrying someone while I was who I was, meant we needed to be forthcoming. The thought of doing so made my trigger finger itch.

"And then..." his tone matched the energy I was giving off. "You will do what's expected of you."

"And?" I asked again, a little more forceful this time.

He narrowed his eyes at me, but that look did nothing to stop where this was headed. I had accepted my fate the minute it was tossed at me, but I would not give up all I'd worked for to satisfy the men in this room.

Never.

There was still too much for me to do—too many things at stake.

"They don't know, do they?"

I glanced at my brother, whose sullen demeanor told me all I needed to know.

"Absolutely not," I said, shaking my head. "You know what will happen if I don't disclose the truth before marrying him."

No organization would be able to withstand the full weight of the Society's wrath if I broke code. My gaze drifted to Enzo and Matteo, who both looked intrigued by my outright disobedience.

"So, who's going to tell him?"

"Tell me what?" Enzo asked, pushing off the wall in a way that commanded the room.

Interesting.

Enzo had been hiding his true self, dimming the power he wielded simply from standing at his full height. He walked toward me and lowered himself into the seat to my left, his gaze on my father.

"It looks like we have more to discuss."

Angelo hadn't moved to stop where this conversation was headed, allowing his heir to do what he'd been bred to.

"A discussion is the lesser of what needs to be done," my father offered, leaning back in his seat.

Leonardo Moretti was a fierce man; he didn't take well to disrespect or being questioned. Enzo, once again, reduced himself out of respect for my father's position, softening the blow.

Smart man, I thought.

From this interaction alone, I saw a leader—a mafioso who deserved to head up a family of his own.

"Your father wanted to have this conversation with you, but because my daughter..." he looked at me, a sprinkle of pride dancing in his eyes. "...has a strong personality. I see we'll be having it now. Show him."

Enzo turned, giving me his rapt attention as I removed my watch and revealed the tattoo hiding beneath it. The simple design—a line that circled my wrist with a single red dot connecting both ends—had a deeper meaning. Most would have no clue what it meant but a *made man*? If smart would know just enough to see the signs.

He didn't speak for a moment; only after his brother approached and whistled in understanding did he reach for my wrist. His touch startled me, a reaction I knew no one else in the room noticed but him. He met my gaze briefly and then turned my wrist over, brushing his thumb over my pulse point.

"This answers my question," he said, still lightly gripping my wrist. "You know how to do more than just handle that gun."

Was that a joke?

I had a lot of talents; reading people is one of them, but Enzo Bianchi was a hard adversary.

"Yeah, she can kill you if need be," Matteo said sardonically, earning a glare from his brother.

"I assume you know how this works."

"I know what I'm allowed to know," he said, pressing his thumb into my pulse point again before releasing me altogether.

"Which is why I need to know what's next," I said, looking at my father and then his. "I'm not stopping."

"But you have the option to," Angelo stated.

He was right. Marrying a made man, let alone one who would be the head of his family one day gave me endless outs from The Red Society.

"An option I don't plan on taking."

They would have to drag me out of here after a fight for their lives to get me to agree.

"Let me address your concerns," Enzo proposed as if he were somehow reading my mind. "Can we have the room?"

"That isn't—"

"Ten minutes," my father agreed, cutting Luca off before he could get his argument out.

My brother and I shared a bond not one person in this room would ever be able to understand. His disparagement for the turn of events was palpable as he and Dante made their exit ahead of our father, Matteo, and Angelo.

The moment the door closed, leaving Enzo and me alone, he stood. I did the same because my training taught me to never allow a man or woman the upper hand in any situation.

He leaned against my father's cherry oak wood desk and crossed his arms, his eyes focused solely on me. I held his gaze, waiting patiently for him to speak.

Patience was a virtue, and I had a lot of it to give despite my wild temper at times.

Chapter 2
Enzo Bianchi

Lucia Moretti blew into her father's office with an air to her only a certain kind of woman could possess. She was sure of herself, and her confidence rivaled that of my own.

I knew I was in for a ride when she stepped into the room in her sinfully high heels, tight curls loose and hanging wildly from her head, with a Glock strapped to her hip.

Being here, doing what should never be expected of any human being, was infuriating enough. Having a wife who was afraid of her own shadow would've been hard to accept for a man like me. I can admit that I'm not the gentlest, and another would be more suited for dealing with a woman who required a softer approach. I'd been single for most of my adult life—only indulging in discreet sexual relationships—for that reason amongst many more.

The jury was still out on how I'd handle having a wife that killed for a living.

"You aren't exactly what I expected," I said, deadly serious in my assumption.

She smirked, her full lips rising at the corners as she moved to stand behind the chairs stationed in front of her father's desk. It was a methodical move, putting something between us in case things went left. I smirked inwardly at that.

"Not being what people expect is my specialty," Lucia quipped, her dark brown eyes dancing.

Her lithe frame was defined in all the right places, making it hard not to notice the way the muscles in her arms peeked through after she folded them. I couldn't help looking her over again, really taking in her features.

I knew she would be beautiful.

I'd seen photos of her, but they'd been at least a few years old. Because of that, I made up my mind that they weren't doing the mafia princess any justice.

The problem was... she was *more* than beautiful.

Lucia's lips were full and painted a deep red color; her eyes were large and dark and lined dramatically. I wasn't sure if she was trying to hide something behind the dramatics of her eye makeup, but it only made me take another long hard look. There were stories no one had ever heard in them—deep shadows that were wary of the people in this world. *Wary of me.*

"You don't want to quit," I said, focusing my attention on her and not how her irises spoke to me.

I knew what her answer would be.

The Red Society bred an elite group of assassins that could be contracted out to any and every crime syndicate in the world. There were rumors of some being freelancers, vigilantes if you will. Most of their identities were unknown; in fact, until today, I'd never knowingly encountered one. She was an enigma in our world, and now I needed to know everything she did.

"I'm *not* quitting."

She shifted her weight onto the right side of her body, tipping her head to the left while waiting for me to respond. I swept my gaze down the length of her, taking note of the tattoos covering part of her exposed abdomen. The colors were vibrant against her mahogany skin tone, and I wondered what was hidden underneath her clothing.

Eventually, I lifted my eyes to meet hers again. Lucia would ultimately learn that I took my time in everything I did, including having conversations that would affect me or the people around me.

"How would it work with our union?"

"I can't be privy to jobs being taken out on my family. Even though I know all and see all." She shrugged, but her confidence was notable, sexy even. "As for you being my husband, if a hit is requested, they not only have to go through The Delegation but *me*."

The Delegation was our version of the Italian-American Mafia's Commission. Though my family was new to the fold, the unity it bared and with whom would make us the most powerful criminal enterprise on the east coast.

Ordering the death of a made man had to go through the Delegation or Commission first—depending on the family. If granted, the parties taking out the hit had seventy-two hours to make it happen. The consequences that came with failing were grave.

I lifted an eyebrow.

"You?"

She smiled, not an ounce of amusement dancing in her suddenly stormy gaze. I felt my body lean forward in an attempt to see through the haze. Lucia wasn't an easy read—a true challenge to say the least.

"If someone tried to kill my husband or a member of his

family, let alone mine, I'd have a problem with that. Which makes *me* a problem for *them*."

I nodded.

"Okay."

She frowned, the haze clearing instantaneously.

"Okay?"

"I'm not in the business of controlling a woman and her desires." Lucia straightened her stance, standing to her full height in those sexy-ass heels she wore. They elongated her legs, making her curves stand out more.

"Then we won't have any problems."

"You'll have a detail," I added, earning a muddled chuckle.

"Enzo..." she smiled wickedly. "If you put a detail on me while I'm on a job, I'll put them down myself."

I smiled, matching her energy.

"I'd love to see it," I told her seriously.

The door to the office opened before she could rebut, her brother and his future consigliere Dante stepping inside moments later.

"Time's up," Luca announced, stating the fucking obvious.

He didn't care for me, but I didn't have an issue with that. This was his sister—his twin, more importantly. Being friends with the man wasn't a goal of mine, and as long as he respected me, I would continue to do the same in return.

I pushed off the desk and reached into the breast pocket of my suit jacket, making everyone but Lucia stiffen. Ignoring her guard dogs, I walked through the opening of the chairs she still stood behind, stopping directly in front of her but leaving a small space between the tips of our shoes. With my eyes trained on hers, I flipped open the ring box in my hand and pulled the two-point five-carat oval diamond ring on a thin gold band from inside.

Lucia dropped her gaze after I grabbed her left hand and slipped the ring onto her finger. I lifted it and admired picking out the right size without needing assistance.

"Looks better than I imagined," I surmised, releasing her.

She looked at me, her true feelings hidden behind another dark cloud. But, I knew something was stirring—call it a hunch if you will. I moved around her toward the door, briefly looking over my shoulder before leaving.

"I'll see you in a week."

I left them to their devices and met my brother at the end of the long corridor. He wore a stupid ass smirk on his face that chafed at my nerves, which was the asshole's goal. Matteo somehow managed to turn everything into a joke, but it was all a show. He wasn't exactly the type to find much of anything funny; I'd seen a man lose an eye for simply thinking he could join in on the roasting.

"Don't start," I warned, leaving the Moretti estate with my personal guard on our heels.

"Your wife is a fucking *Red*, Enzo," he mused, lifting his head to our guards standing outside the Moretti estate, signaling them to fall back and wait for our father.

We moved down the drive toward our bulletproof black-on-black Escalade. Behind it was our father's matching truck and another meant solely for the guards that followed us here.

I took the wheel while Matteo slipped into the passenger seat, and the single guard we kept with us at all times—while away from our territory—got into the back.

"I heard the same conversation as you," I said, pulling toward the gate and idling for a short moment while it opened, and the outside of our vehicle was checked. "She'll be useful."

"Unless she takes you out in your sleep."

"I would love to see her try."

"Me too," he said. "Call if it comes to that, I'll have popcorn on standby at all times."

I ignored him and looked into the rearview mirror, meeting the eyes of Malik. He only stayed focused on me for a second before looking around for any threats.

I placed my eyes back on the road and asked, "Anything from back home?"

He shook his head, never one to speak unless he had valuable information.

Before leaving Grayfall, we learned that someone shot Pietro Costa Junior—the Costa crime family's throne heir. While the attempt hadn't been fatal, the Costas were pulling in as many resources as they could to find the person ballsy enough to do it.

"I want everyone on high alert."

I didn't give a fuck about him being shot.

In fact, if he'd been put down, it would've lightened the load I currently had on my shoulders. The Costas were pests, the scum of the earth—bottom fucking feeders who didn't believe in following the code.

They were into some shit we didn't agree with. None of us claimed to be good people, we were all knee-deep in illegal dealings, but there were some trades you stayed away from.

"Fucking scum," I cursed. "All of 'em."

Seeing my mood shift, Matteo pulled his phone out and found something else to occupy the time it would take us to get back to New Jersey from Pennsylvania. It was a short drive for someone who'd done it more times than I could count, but long enough to reflect on the drastic changes forced upon us after our grandfather's death.

Alessandro Bianchi had been one of the five heads of the Italian-American mafia. He and our grandmother Martina hadn't been able to have their own children, so they adopted—

our father being the first brought into the fold at just six months old.

While our *nonna* was a caring woman with a heart larger than life, that brute she'd been forced to marry was no such thing. He'd eventually fallen in love, and that alone was the motivation behind him allowing a *Black* baby into the family. The details behind my father's adoption were scarce, but they'd somehow ended up with him.

Nonno needed to have an heir—one that looked like the rest of them, so they'd adopted again four years later. Our uncle Giovanni now sat at the head of the family.

It was a position that rightfully belonged to our father—a position our *Zio* snatched from right under him on the pretenses of appearance. Our father was not only a Black man, but he'd refused to marry a good full-blooded Italian woman, instead choosing his childhood love—a woman who had been born in Italy to Afro-Italian emigrants.

With that, our *Zio* had the ammunition he needed to unload the clip in his favor without remorse. The family backed him, spewing their lies about love and loyalty to us along the way. Something our father had given to them wholeheartedly his entire life, but that was over now. We'd been tossed aside for all intents and purposes, given titles that meant nothing in the grand scheme of things—not when you were raised to be leaders.

We were on our own now—relinquishing all titles with the nod from the Commission to do so—and had been for the last six months. Any business or alliances we'd made were no longer a part of *their* mafia. My father had prepared for this, making us strong enough to stand on our own, but we were smart enough to know that strength came in numbers. And what better way to show ours than by tying ourselves with another family who'd been more or less tossed aside for the same reason?

"Loosen your grip before the steering wheel breaks, Enz," Matteo suggested, his fingers moving rapidly over his phone's keyboard. "Everything will fall into place."

I released the warm leather and sighed. He was right and always the voice of reason in these instances where my anger began to get the best of me. For that reason, Matteo would be my consigliere when I took over for our father.

"Giovanni asked to meet," he went on. "I told him to go fuck himself."

My lips spread, knowing he'd done no such thing.

"Seems our little birdy did her job," I said.

Speaking of said birdy, I answered the call coming through on the truck's Bluetooth system.

"Don't ever ask me to do that again," Gia fumed, her usual soft tone raised slightly. "I hate her."

"Bluebird," Matteo cooed, making our sister more upset by using that stupid nickname. "She's our cousin."

"Kiara is not my *cugina*," Gia cursed, spitting the word out in Italian. "You two can claim that witch, but I refuse. Besides, those people aren't our family. We are all we got."

Gia was soft on the outside but complete chaos internally. She was a true Bianchi through and through—at least in name. Genetically we were nothing like our family, not sharing their DNA in every sense of the word. But whoever our father's biological parents were had to have wild spirits and tempers bigger than life because our mother and maternal grandparents were no such thing.

"We won't make you do that ever again," I told her. "Your service is appreciated."

"Mmhm," she hummed. "How's the new wife?"

"Fiancée," I corrected.

"Same difference. She's the reason Zio is currently calling every person in the family looking for any information they have on her." She chuckled. "You should've seen his face after Kiara defied my trust—just as I suspected she would—and called him into the room to announce the exciting news."

Matteo and I exchanged glances.

Now that we knew what we did about Lucia, no one else could ever find out.

"I have to go," she said, already done with the conversation and us. "Some of us are getting college degrees and have homework."

She ended the call, and Matteo mumbled, "I don't know if I should be offended or proud."

"You have a college degree," I reminded him.

We both did, which Gianna was aware of.

"Have an invite to the wedding sent to Giovanni. He's allowed to bring his wife, daughter, and a guard for each of them if he chooses. Any more than that can wait outside the gates of the Moretti estate."

Matteo chuckled while typing out the message to whoever would be handling the invites with glee.

"I need two guards on Lucia at all times," I went on, talking to Malik. My mind began to work in overdrive as we approached the casino we owned in Grayfall, New Jersey. "Tell them to be as invisible as they can, or she will kill them."

He nodded, his eyes moving from left to right before meeting mine in the mirror while he reached for his phone.

"Are you sure about that?" Matteo asked. "We can't afford to hire and train new guards if she offs them, not when we're still building allies."

I believed her threat when she'd dished it, but that wouldn't stop me from protecting her, even if she was trained to do just that for herself. Once you were under my protection—in my family, I took it seriously.

"Replace them now."

"We might need to replace *you* once she figures it out." He reached for the radio knob. "And I'm almost certain she *will* figure it out."

I was banking on it.

Lucia had my attention, and I wanted to press every button she possessed until I found the one that would set her off—giving me a glimpse into the person she kept hidden under lock and key. My lips curved at the thought that maybe having a wife wouldn't be so bad. Especially one of her caliber.

I pulled up to the private parking garage of the casino, stopping close enough for the magnetic strip installed in the bumper to be scanned. The steel door lifted, and I cruised through, pulling into my designated parking place seconds later.

"I have some shit to handle," Matteo said after we all exited. He walked over to his burnt orange Lamborghini truck and hit the locks, pulling the driver's side door open and slipping inside. "I'll be around in a few hours if you need anything; my phone is on me."

He shut the door and waited for Malik to finish checking his truck for bugs.

Once he finished, he nodded to my brother, who all but peeled out of the garage.

Malik did the same with the Escalade even though we'd been checked before entering and leaving the Moretti estate. To us, none of that mattered; anything was possible, and because of that, we needed to be vigilant.

"You can head up to the security suite; I'm good from here."

He gave me a look that I'd grown accustomed to over the years whenever I ordered he went about his business away from me. I opened my suit jacket revealing the gun strapped to my waist and then pulled my left pant leg up slightly to reveal my favorite knife and a gun connected to my ankle.

I walked toward the elevator that would take me directly to the casino, while Malik reluctantly took the elevator that would lead him to the security level. When I turned, just as the doors were closing, I caught him peering over his shoulder at me, still watching my back with just us two around. He was a good soldier, loyal to us and only us.

The elevator took me up one level, and I stepped off into a corridor. Out of the corner of my eyes, I caught my cousin on my mother's side and the casino manager—Brandon—moving quickly toward me.

"Just in time," he muttered as he passed and pulled open a door that led to a tunneled walkway. "You might want to follow me."

I peered through the glass door onto the casino's main floor and then turned away, letting my body carry me over to Brandon. I lifted an eyebrow in question, and he answered without needing to be prompted.

"We caught him."

Ah.

I moved through the secured door—that could only be opened by a handful of people who had their thumbprint uploaded for access—and across the walkway toward the mini high-rise building on the other side. There were ten floors; the top three were apartments—two of them belonging to Matteo and me and the other waiting to be given to Gia as a graduation gift. While the six floors below us housed a data lab, gym, two private medical suites staffed with medical professionals on my payroll, and two security levels that monitored the comings and goings of the casino, hotel, and everything surrounding it. The main floor had a lobby where a guard and doorman were stationed at all times. Below that was the basement, where Brandon and I were headed.

"Slow down," Brandon complained, trying to keep up. "We aren't all in shape."

I reached the other side and pressed my thumb into the scanner connected to the door handle. The locks disengaged, and I stepped through, Brandon on my heels.

Turning, I looked into his flushed face.

"There's a gym you have access to and refuse to use," I pointed out dryly. "How'd you figure it out?"

"He was in the middle of exchanging with the new blackjack dealer. I went back to view the cameras, and he's been meeting the same woman for months now, every Monday."

I cursed in Italian.

Dealing drugs in my casino was against every policy I had in place to keep it from happening but selling it to the people who worked for me was a death sentence. Anyone in a hundred-mile radius of Grayfall knew it, yet it kept fucking happening.

Nothing about me or my lifestyle made me a good man, but I prided myself on giving people second chances. Because of that, a select few of my staff had some sort of addiction at one time in their life. It was a violation of my trust and the casino's code of conduct to partake in any selling or buying of a substance—meaning their drug of choice.

"And the girl from before?"

Over the last month, I had three of my staff overdose while off the clock—one doing so inside of a bathroom in the casino a few nights ago.

"She's in stable condition."

I nodded and pulled off my jacket, handing it to him. Brandon draped it over his arm and took his leave as I made my way down. It was dark, but I knew my way without needing the guidance of light. The whimpers of a man crying out filled the space around us, fueling the anger brewing inside me for months now.

"The more you cry, the more damage he'll do," I said, making myself known.

Rocco turned, with an evil smile on his face. His thick locs were pulled into a man bun on top of his head, the sleeves of his dress shirt rolled up but spotted with blood. He had a bulky frame and the speed of a running back. In fact, he'd played the position in college where I'd met him. Turned out that Rocco had a violent streak, and I just so happened to have a use for men like him.

"Bossman," he greeted, his grin widening. "I decided to warm him up for you."

I rolled my sleeves up and crossed the room, staring into the now wide eyes of a man who once had my trust.

Joseph had been my head of security at the casino for over five years, and while I was only twenty-nine years old, I still believed myself to be a good judge of character. So to learn that a man I put my trust in wasn't doing his job to the best of his ability pissed me the fuck off.

"E-Enzo, I swear to God—"

"Don't swear to God in my presence," I snapped, pulling at my tie and tossing it to Rocco. "God can't save you down here."

"I-I didn't—"

"All I've ever asked of you was that you protect everyone employed at the casino..." I crossed my arms and sighed. "and you did the complete opposite by putting them in harm's way. A mother of two who was having a hard time in life came to us for help, and instead of getting that, she was given exactly what she'd been afraid of."

I still believed in those old-school rules that innocent women and children were off-limits, and that innocent people, in general, didn't deserve to be dragged into somebody else's bullshit, but everyone didn't see things the Bianchi 2.0 way.

I lifted my gaze to meet his.

"I don't care to hear your pleas or excuses." I circled the chair he was tied to. "Here's how this will go, Joseph. You can either point me in the direction of your supplier, or I'll let Rocco take another swing at you."

He whimpered at the mention of his attacker, whipping his head from side to side.

"You know I have a family."

I *tsked* and lowered myself in front of him.

"I don't have beef with your family." I took the blade Rocco held out for me and stuck its tip into the wound he'd been working at when I arrived, splitting his skin open more and then shoving it in deeper. "My issues lie with you and you alone. Not only did you break my trust, but you endangered my business."

He'd allowed this mystery woman into my casino, into our security room.

The betrayal was thick.

Joseph's cries grew as I prodded the hole in his leg, watching blood pool around the blade. He cried out a name that I didn't quite catch and shoved the blade deeper.

"Who!"

"Mariana," he screamed. "Her name is Mariana Costa! That's all I know, I swear. S-She offered—"

"Shut the fuck up!"

I snatched the mostly covered steel from the gaping wound, wiped it off on his torn shirt, and returned it to Rocco. Standing, I grabbed the gun on my hip and aimed it right between his eyes.

"Please—"

"You should've thought of the consequences before

teaming up with the likes of a *Costa*," I spat, gripping the trigger and then pulling.

I tucked my gun and turned to Rocco.

"Have someone else get rid of him. Find his family, and then find Mariana Costa!"

"How much?" he asked as I turned for the exit.

"Whatever it takes to get people talking. I want answers one way or another, Roc."

Grayfall was like no other city in the United States. Every section of it was owned by some form of a crime syndicate, and then there were the regular people who worked normal jobs that lived in the middle of it all, turning a blind eye to what they witnessed on a daily.

We could force them to talk, but what's a better incentive than enough money to move your family somewhere safer? Especially when the people meant to protect were just as dirty.

The Grayfall Police Department was as corrupt as they come. The elected officials were connected to the underworld in more ways than one. *Everyone* had a chip on their shoulder—my family with the biggest one of all. So, if a little bribe could save just one innocent family from the chaos of this city, then maybe God would find it in his heart to forgive me for the life I lived.

Chapter 3

Lucia

"Your phone again." Gaia turned it to face me while I continued to adjust my clothing at the boutique's entrance we were on our way out of. We'd been able to find my wedding dress rather quickly, and today Gaia came with me while I tried on the altered product.

I glanced at the screen and shook my head.

"Ignore it, and let's go."

The men in my life were collectively working at my last nerve on purpose.

It had to be the only logical explanation for my brother calling me nonstop in the days following our meeting with Enzo and his family—only to never have anything important to say.

Don't even get me started on Enzo fucking Bianchi.

He went against my request not to have a detail on me. I'd caught on to them the minute I pulled off my parent's estate and made it to my condo the night we met. Four days later and they were still following me. Granted, they were trying to be as invisible as possible. Still, even the most trained man would have difficulty getting past my attentive nature.

My threat to put them down would've stood if I'd been on the job. But because I'd been subjected to multiple shopping days with my mother, aunt, and cousin Gaia, I decided to let it slide. The idea of them suffering through this type of torture was enough of a punishment.

"How will we handle the safe house situation if you have a permanent detail following you around?"

I wouldn't admit it to her just yet, but I'd been stressing about our operation the last few days. It was bigger than just taking out the Costa family—bigger than ridding the world of filth like them. Victims were involved, who needed protection, and now that I had more responsibility being thrown at me, I had to improvise.

"Don't worry your pretty little head about that. I have a failsafe in place. There's no getting out of this whole marriage thing, but that's why we have a solid team, G."

"Care to include me in this plan of yours?"

I smiled.

"Ask me that question you loved when we were younger."

Gaia narrowed her eyes at me, but after a few seconds, she knew.

"Should we feed them?" Gaia asked, looping her arm through mine. "If they're always watching you, when do they eat? How is it that I still don't have an answer to that after all these years."

I chuckled and scanned the area around us out of habit. We were without our mothers, making it a less stressful day for all parties and the perfect opportunity to get into some trouble.

While not *technically* a part of this lifestyle, Gaia was my right hand in business, best friend, and cousin. My mother was also her godmother, and we spent a lot of time together growing up.

She was my ride or die.

"Why don't we find out?" I asked, a smile pulling at my lips.

"Oh no," she muttered under her breath as I began to pull her down Venice Drive toward their car. "We don't have to—"

I knocked on the tinted window and leaned back just as it began to roll down. Sitting in the passenger seat wasn't anyone I recognized from a few nights ago, but I knew they were Enzo's men. I ducked my head into the window slightly and met the eyes of the driver, noting that neither of them had spoken.

"Do you two eat?" I asked, casually reaching for the Glock sitting on the passenger's lap.

He didn't stop me, and I smiled, twisting the pistol from side to side. I had an obsession with guns. It started when I was about twelve, and my shot was pristine—better than my brother's by the time I was fourteen.

"Do we eat?" the driver asked, his brows furrowed.

I set the gun back where I'd gotten it and lifted my gaze.

"Yes. Food. Do you eat it?" I tipped my head back toward Gaia. "My cousin seems to think you two don't eat since you've been following us for four days, to be exact."

"We—"

"Lucia—"

"Is it not true?" I questioned, turning to find her eyebrows lifted.

She hated being put on the spot, but I was on a roll and would make it up to her later. I turned back to my guards, both of who looked younger than me, but looks could be deceiving.

"What are your names?"

"Gastone," the driver said.

I looked to his partner, who replied with, "Orlando."

"Alright, Gastone and Orlando. I'm Lucia, and this is Gaia."

They looked too stunned to speak, but I didn't have a problem with that because no words were needed for what we were about to do.

"Take us to Grayfall," I requested, stepping back and pulling open the back door.

I waved for Gaia to get in.

"Grayfall," she repeated slowly, blinking at me as if I were crazy. "You want them to take us to New Jersey? Are you out of —never mind."

She knew better than anyone that I was quite literally unhinged at times. This hadn't been the plan but now that the idea had taken root inside of my mind, taking no for an answer wasn't possible.

"You can take my truck back to the condo if you don't feel comfortable."

She rolled her pretty brown eyes but slid into the backseat like I'd known she would.

I smiled and climbed in behind her.

"Ms.—"

"Call me Lucia," I corrected, buckling my seat belt.

"Lucia, we'll have to call Enzo. He expects regular updates."

I shrugged.

"It's better he be prepared for my arrival."

Gastone pulled away from the curb, and Gaia leaned between the two seats.

"So, how much do you get paid to babysit?" she asked, not caring that she'd just called two made men *babysitters*.

I snorted.

"Be nice, G."

She cut her eyes at me over her shoulder, a bright smile playing on her nude-tinted lips.

"I am being nice." She turned back. "So... how much?"

Neither of them answered, but it wouldn't deter her. I almost felt sorry for them, but the feeling only lasted a few seconds before disappearing.

"The silent types," she mused, sitting back. "Don't worry, I'll get you talking soon."

I chuckled and stared out the window as we merged onto the interstate, tuning out Gaia's voice. As the distance from the place I'd known my entire life grew, I felt my freedom being snatched from me. *Piece by piece.*

In a few days, my life would be in the hands of a man I knew nothing of. Men like my father, brother, and Enzo were born leaders, naturally expecting the people around them to conform to their lives and daily moves. While I respected their roles in our society, I had a hard time with authority in general.

Enzo Bianchi was the epitome of power, even when he tried downplaying it.

Placing myself on his stomping grounds before we were official to those around us was a test for all involved. How far could I push the underboss before he tried putting his foot down and controlling me?

I smiled at the thought.

"I know that look," Gaia said, taking my hand and lacing our fingers together. "You don't have to be tough all the time."

I cut my eyes at her.

"Says who?"

"Me! And I know my stuff."

"Mmhm."

I wouldn't discuss this with her while having eyes and ears on us that weren't loyal to me. Whatever was said in this vehicle would be reported to Enzo, giving him something to use against me if needed. I shook off the dark thoughts racing through my mind—now wasn't the time to spiral.

"How far out are we?" I asked, glancing at my watch.

We'd been driving for about forty minutes.

"Fifteen minutes," Gastone answered.

"He's expecting you at the casino," Orlando added, reminding me that he'd informed him of my impromptu visit.

"Casino?" Gaia questioned, turning to me.

I guess I hadn't been as forthcoming about my future husband.

"His family owns two, and Enzo oversees the one in Grayfall with his brother," I told her. "The other is in Atlantic City."

She hummed in understanding.

The things I'd learned about him—what he'd allowed out there for the people to gossip about—pointed to him being both street and book smart. He was levelheaded in public, but I sensed a bit of a temper that I found myself wanting to experiment with.

We pulled off the interstate, and Gaia released my hand, her eyes scanning the semi-empty streets. Grayfall was a lot like Blackthorne—half the city destitute while the other side housed the wealthy and corrupt.

"Is that it?"

She pointed, and I followed her gaze, taking in the two buildings connected by a tunneled walkway—one with a large sign on the side of the building that read: *The Myriad Casino and Hotel*.

Gastone pulled the car to a steel door that lifted the closer he got, allowing him to drive straight through and into what looked to be a private parking garage. He parked next to a row of Escalades and smaller sedans like the one we were in.

Orlando hopped out the minute we stopped and opened

my door before I had the chance to. I nodded and walked around him to take in our surroundings.

"This way," Gastone called, walking toward an elevator.

Gaia glanced at me and then shrugged, following behind him without a second thought. On the other hand, I waited until Orlando began to move to do the same. We migrated into the elevator and silently took it one floor up. The doors opened, and Gastone once again took the lead, with Orlando following directly behind us. He turned to the right, but I kept straight, pulling open the double doors to the casino floor.

"Lucia," Gaia called, catching up to me. "What are you—oh wow."

The casino was packed, bodies moving collectively from table to table.

There was nothing special about the space; it looked like a typical casino—darkened to fulfill a certain mood with slot machines and tables where blackjack and other games were being played.

"Who the hell wants to lose money this bad?" she questioned softly, speaking my thoughts aloud. "They do know these institutions are meant to take and not give, right?"

I took my time walking through, taking in the dealers who were dressed in all black.

"People are staring."

I could feel their eyes but being stared at was something I'd grown accustomed to. People tended to sense when you were somebody important, especially in a town like this. I knew Gastone and Orlando were following us, making our presence more noticeable.

Smiling, I stopped at a roulette table and slipped into an empty seat.

"A pretty woman who likes roulette," the gentleman beside

me spoke, a cigarette hanging from his lips. His gaze landed on Gaia next. "*Two* pretty women."

"Two pretty women who hate the smell of these cancer sticks you are smoking," Gaia said, taking it from his lips and putting it out. "Light it up when we're gone."

"You can't—"

"I can and did," she told him, cutting into whatever he'd been about to say.

He looked behind us and then pressed his lips together before looking away.

Smart man.

I slid the dealer two one hundred dollar bills for the hell of it. I wasn't a gambler; losing money didn't appease me. Not when I could be spending it on a new gun instead of lining the pockets of someone else. But seeing as I'd have a stake in this place one day, I wanted to try my luck. Roulette so happened to be a game my cousin, and I liked.

The dealer—a fair-skinned woman with large eyes—slid four chips worth twenty-five dollars each my way and placed the other four in front of Gaia after tilting my head toward her. We both moved to place our bets before she could begin; I went straight up—placing one chip on five black and one on thirty red.

Gaia split—like always—placing a chip between red twenty-one and black twenty-four. We cut our eyes at one another and then back on the board, placing chips on each other's bets while everyone around us skeptically placed their own.

"No more bets," the dealer called as the ball in the roulette wheel began to slow.

"Text Jaz," I muttered to Gaia. "Tell her to move, and I'll explain later."

She nodded and pulled her phone out, quickly sending off the text.

The ball bounced for a few short moments before landing on red thirty. The dealer announced the number, placed the puck on top of our chips, and swept the board of the rest. As the dealer paid us our winnings, the air on the floor changed.

I didn't need to turn and gawk with the rest of the room; I felt his energy and knew he was closing the distance between us in long, sure strides. Smirking, I leaned over and placed my chips onto my neighbor's pile. His eyes widened, and my lips spread wider.

"For being a good sport," I said, standing and turning to face my fiancé.

His gaze swept the length of me, and I did the same to him, taking note of his casual attire and tattoo-covered arms. Custom-made suits were like a uniform to a mafia man. You rarely saw them without one, but this man... wasn't your typical *mafioso*.

"Enjoying yourself?" he asked as I closed the distance between us.

I shrugged.

"Not the gambling type."

He lifted an eyebrow and leaned forward.

"Yet, here you are."

"Here I am."

"And me too," Gaia said, slipping in beside me. "I'm her favorite cousin in the entire world."

The expression on his face never changed, but he acknowledged her statement with a slight incline of his head.

"Gaia, right?" he questioned.

She nodded and tipped her head to the side, eyeing him curiously.

"Do you mind if I borrow your cousin? We need to have a word, but I won't keep her long."

His gaze met mine briefly before he placed it on Gaia once more, genuinely wanting her blessing. I was almost hoping she demanded to come along, but the girl betrayed me with ease.

"I'm good here," she said, watching me from the corner of her eyes.

He nodded at Orlando and Gastone and then reached for my hand, taking it into his and strategically pressing his thumb into my pulse point—a move that seemed natural to him.

I allowed him to lead us, my eyes meeting Gaia's wide gaze. "He's beautiful," she mouthed, fanning herself.

I rolled my eyes and turned away, needing to keep up with his quick pace. We walked in silence, exiting the casino floor and taking a right toward a door.

"It can only be opened with a thumbprint," he said, twisting the handle after allowing his to be scanned. "While you're here, I'll have yours uploaded for access."

I didn't respond, only quietly following his lead into the walkway I'd spotted when we arrived. We made it quickly to the other side, where another set of elevators sat. He didn't explain, and I didn't ask any questions as we stepped on, and he pressed a button with an E etched into it. The doors closed, and then he turned, his eyes staring what felt like deeply into my soul.

"See something you like?" I asked, not being able to help myself.

He chuckled, and it vibrated through me, filling my body with urges I fought hard to mask.

"I see a lot I like, actually," he muttered, licking his full lips. "But that's neither here nor there." He stepped closer. "You got something you need to say to me?"

I lifted an eyebrow.

"You got into a car with two men you couldn't be a thousand percent sure were my men, and now here we are, standing in this elevator face to face. Is that what you wanted?"

The elevator halted, and the doors slid open before I could respond. I looked over his shoulder into a large apartment. Because I needed room to breathe, I ducked under his arm and stepped inside the aesthetically dark penthouse.

The open floor plan allowed me to take in the living, dining room, and kitchen in one long sweep. His place was modern and decorated in dark earth tones—black, dark olive green, and subtle splashes of various shades of brown. It felt like a home, which surprised me because I'd entirely expected something else.

I moved further into his domain and grazed the picture frames with the tips of my fingers. Then, I did the same with his delicate art pieces before stopping in front of the floor-to-ceiling length windows.

"They're bulletproof," he said, his tone soft but deep enough to carry.

I schooled my labored breathing as best I could before speaking.

"I knew they were your men," I said, eyeing the array of colors in the sky as the sun began to set over the Atlantic. "I told you I miss nothing."

I turned, and there he was, right up on me—his body close enough for me to reach out and touch, something I had to stop myself from doing.

"Thank you for sparing them."

His praise surprised me, but I tried playing it cool by shrugging.

"I wasn't on the job."

"No..." he shook his head, a ghost of a smile playing on his lips. "Just shopping. Something I wouldn't have guessed to be your thing."

I snorted.

"It isn't," I confirmed. "I prefer browsing online with a glass of wine in hand."

He hummed in response, his gaze searching mine for nothing, in particular.

"Why'd you ask to be brought here?"

"Is this where we'll be living?"

How could I give a truthful reply when I didn't know the answer my damn self?

Sure I was using this as a way to give my team time to take care of business but coming here hadn't needed to happen in order for that to be done. What had felt like a good idea at the time didn't feel that way anymore. I wasn't an impulsive being; everything I did had a reason. Yet, here I was—in his neck of the woods for no damn reason.

"It is," he said, going along with my change of subject. "My brother is on the floor below us, and the one below that will belong to our sister closer to the end of the year. The rest I'll show you another day."

I nodded slowly, looking away from him and at everything around us instead.

"Show me around," I requested, moving to brush past him only to be stopped.

He grabbed my arm and curled his fingers lightly around my wrist to keep me in place. I stared down at where our skin connected, then up at him.

"You're getting a little too comfortable touching me without my permission."

The words tasted bitter on my tongue, a telltale sign that my body didn't appreciate the bullshit lie I'd spewed. Truthfully, I didn't like being touched. I tolerated it, but the handful of times he'd had me in his grasp, my body reacted in ways that were foreign to my psyche.

I think I *liked* it when *he* touched me and that alone was too much for me to handle.

"You're right," he agreed, releasing and leaving me in disbelief. "Forgive me for overstepping."

I narrowed my eyes, not sure if I should believe the gentleman act. My experience with men who weren't related to me had never been pleasant. When you're the daughter of a powerful man and find your place in a world where women aren't generally accepted, you tend to encounter asshole after asshole. I'd been tested on many occasions and, in return, shattered a few egos, making enemies out of a lot of my counterparts.

Enzo's intentions were a mystery to me, and I didn't like going into situations blind. This union was as blind as they came, and it spiked my fight-or-flight instincts. I opened my mouth to announce that I needed to get back to Gaia, but the elevator doors opened and cut into that.

My reaction to the unexpected guest was to reach for the gun tucked under my blouse. I pulled and pointed it before my mind could catch up to my actions.

Fight or flight.

"What the fuck," the man yelped after being greeted by my gun pointed at his head.

He looked between Enzo and me, then lifted his hands. A sign that he was a friendly—an ally. Even knowing that, something inside of my body wouldn't allow me to lower my weapon.

"Brandon," Enzo greeted, his tone clipped. "Meet my fiancée Lucia."

Enzo reached out and pushed my hand down.

"He's my cousin. You can relax."

"I didn't mean to interrupt," Brandon said, shifting nervously. "Uh…"

He paused and looked at me, a move that immediately pissed me off. Not the action per se but the meaning behind it. It was a silent question.

Can she hear this? He'd asked it with his eyes.

Brandon was nothing like Enzo; he was easily scared and even easier to read.

"Speak."

His eyes narrowed at Enzo's demand.

Mmm.

Maybe he wasn't easily scared, after all, just caught off guard by me. Though he'd looked at his cousin with a *what the fuck was that* expression, he spoke quickly after.

"Your uncle is here. He requested to speak to your father, but as you know—"

"He isn't here," Enzo finished, a hint of annoyance there. "Which he knows."

Brandon nodded.

"Should—"

The elevator doors opened, and the man I knew to be Giovanni Bianchi stepped inside the apartment with two guards on his heels. Enzo's body stiffened—a reaction I shouldn't have expected but did. I could feel his disdain for the man, and it put me on high alert.

I didn't know the full story about the quiet falling out he and his extended family had, only what they'd allowed everyone to think—that it was a mutual separation. Nothing about this mini-reunion pointed to that.

"Giovanni, have you ever heard of calling first?" Enzo asked, moving forward.

I unconsciously followed him, tucking my gun behind my back as I did.

"You're a hard man to get in touch with these days, *Nipote*."

I snorted at his use of the word Nephew. He'd said it like it were a curse word—spitting it out harder than the rest of his statement. Giovanni was one of those Italian men with an inferiority problem through and through—the olive skin, slicked-back hair, and beady eyes drove my point home. His spirit was ugly, which made me stand closer to Enzo.

Protectively?

I shook that thought away.

Giovanni spared me a dismissive glance, just as many men in his position did on a regular. And as I expected, he turned back because I wasn't a bitch you could simply dismiss without doing a double-take.

"Lucia Moretti," he surmised his left brow lifting. "I see I interrupted something."

"In the flesh," I confirmed, smiling. "You didn't interrupt much. I'm simply getting acquainted with my future husband." I slipped my fingers through Enzo's, who hadn't done anything to stop me from speaking—*bonus points to you, hubby*. "Did you get an invite to the wedding?"

His gaze dropped to our joined fingers, and I fought hard not to laugh.

"We talked about this, *Bellissima*," Enzo spoke, releasing my hand and pulling me deeper into his side. "My *zio* is against not being able to bring more guards with him into the estate."

That was news to me, but I played along, ignoring the swirling in my belly at his fingers digging softly into my side.

"My mother's side of the family doesn't know this life," I explained, sprinkling a little truth into the lie I was about to tell. "Too many armed guards spook them, so we require all guests to leave their men off the grounds. Trust that you and your family will be on neutral territory for the night."

"For the night only?"

He hadn't directed the question at me, and fire replaced the odd swirling in my stomach. I despised being looked over as a source of information. I could easily give him the answer he *wasn't* looking for. A big fat *fuck you* and your safety would suffice.

Somehow feeling my brewing anger, Enzo brushed his hand down my arm. It was enough to distract me, enough to calm me slightly.

"Was there a specific reason you came here?"

"We need to talk..." Giovanni cut his eyes at me. "Another time. When you aren't *distracted*."

He looked over his shoulder, and one of the guards hit the button to call for the elevator. The doors opened immediately; he turned, stopping to eye us over his shoulder.

"It was a pleasure, Ms. Moretti. I will take your word and see you and my nephew in a few days."

Enzo's fingers tightened, and I forced a smile.

He stepped into the elevator, followed by his detail and Brandon. When the doors closed, I cursed in Italian.

"I *do not* like him," I said, pulling myself out of Enzo's hold.

"Glad to know you'll be loyal to me and mine."

I stepped directly in front of him, lifting my eyes to meet his assessing gaze.

"Loyalty should never be a question when it comes to me." Despite my current conflicting feelings, I leaned in close, my nose just barely touching his. "Can I say the same for you?"

Enzo took a deep breath, and when he released it, a low growl escaped.

I took a shuddered breath and the corner of his mouth lifted. His eyes were dark, evil almost, and *that* expression alone was all my clit needed to react.

"Whatever perfume that is, wear it on our wedding day."

"Is that an order?"

He backed away, the smirk gone from his face.

"No, Lucia..." he shook his head and walked over to the elevator, hitting the call button. "It's a request. One that I'm hoping you'll kindly oblige to."

It took a few seconds, but eventually, the doors opened to the elevator, and he slipped his body halfway inside, pausing to wait for me to enter. I stepped forward, angling my frame sideways to slip past him, never making it.

"I need you to understand something," he murmured into my ear after wrapping his arm around my waist and dragging my body against his.

I twisted in an attempt to get out of his grasp, but Enzo's hold on me only tightened, showing his strength. His fingers grazed my gun, and then he gripped it, never once pulling it from the waistband of my jeans yet using it as a way to keep me in place.

"What's that?" I gritted, fighting with too many intense emotions.

I wanted to pounce; he could fuck me right here and now, and I wouldn't stop it. But on the other hand, I wanted to fight; more specifically, I wanted to break his nose with my forehead.

"Playing the dutiful wife in front of guests when I now know you could put everyone out of their misery without blinking only makes me want to fuck you," he confessed.

Breathe, Lucia.

"And?"

"And unless you want to be bent over before our wedding night, then I suggest you keep your distance as much as possible."

He pushed me into the elevator and stepped back into his apartment. I stared at him, my back against the shell of the steel box and my chest rising and falling. His eyes were dark and filled with lust, his jeans tented with proof that he wanted me as bad as it sounded.

And fuck me.

I wanted him, too.

The doors shut, but the last thing I'd seen before they closed completely was a smile so big on his face that it shattered my heart in the best way possible.

This marriage was meant to be in name only—a union to secure more power between our two respective families. To be feeling *something*—whatever this was—before we said *I do* was not normal. Nothing about what had transpired was ordinary.

Enzo Bianchi was going to be a problem—one I'd never be able to get rid of.

A conflict of fucking interest, to say the least.

What the fuck had I agreed to?

I was in a hurry to get out of Grayfall, but that became delayed when I was met by a guard who introduced himself as Malik. He escorted me to be *fingerprinted* and afterward took me down to the parking garage where Gastone, Orlando, and Gaia were waiting.

The drive back to my truck was silent, and I appreciated the reprieve. I needed a moment to gather myself before Gaia, and I got to work. Gastone and Orlando dropped us off and left.

"Are they not following us?"

I shook my head.

Enzo had only done it to get me riled up, having them follow me until I did something about it. He was calling them off because I hadn't reacted as I said I would. *For now.*

"Not this time..."

"Do you want to talk about it?" she asked, changing subjects.

I shook my head and focused on the road, counting down

from ten and then doing it all over again until my heart rate returned to its natural beat. My fingers flexed around the steering wheel.

"Where are they?" I asked, pulling into the storage unit to stash my truck.

"Waiting for us."

I nodded.

We quickly changed and then got into my trusty Honda.

"I hate this death trap. You need to buy a new one."

I rolled my eyes and started it up; the old car purred to life, and I smiled.

"It hasn't steered me wrong yet," I told her. "Worry about your gadgets, and I'll continue to take care of transportation."

She mumbled something under her breath but immediately got to work, pulling out a tracking device shaped like a cell phone. I listened to her tap away until we reached one of our four safe houses.

"They're on the move," she said. "We have ten minutes top to intercept before they're out of the dead zone, or we'll lose this one."

We switched from the Honda to a blacked-out cargo van. Gaia climbed into the back with me while Jaz and Violet—who'd been waiting inside—rode up front.

"Ready?" Jaz called, already driving away.

I felt my body relax, my shoulders dropping as I rolled them to release the tension.

"As ready as we'll ever be," Gaia replied.

I inspected my gun again, checking the clip twice before twisting on the silencer.

"We're coming up on the transport."

Gaia cut her eyes at me, and I nodded, pulling my ski mask down at the same time as her. Jaz increased speed, whipping the van between lanes before tapping the back of the transport we wanted and coming to a hard stop. I could hear the commotion on the outside, the shouts in Italian.

We pushed the back doors open and hopped out, guns drawn. The two men who'd been shouting for Jaz and Violet to get out hadn't seen us coming. There was no time for them to react. I put one round into who I figured to be the driver's head, rushing forward to search his pockets for the key to unlock the back of their van.

Gaia dropped the passenger, and then the four of us worked in sync, dragging their bodies into the back of our van and then driving away in both.

Chapter 4

Enzo

"If it isn't my father, mother, brother, or sister, I don't want them able to get through these fucking doors," I snapped, walking through the tunnel to meet my father. Giovanni showing up at my apartment unannounced and as if he were still welcomed was a bold move that wouldn't be happening again. He'd known exactly what doing it meant, how it would make me feel.

"Your wife, sir?"

My wife.

I halted my stride and glanced over my shoulder at Malik.

She wasn't exactly that yet, but unless one of us somehow ended up dead before the *big* day, she would be soon enough. Lucia had been fingerprinted before leaving—giving her access to every crevice of what will be our home and business.

"You want her to have access to everything?" he clarified.

Without a second thought, I nodded and continued across the walkway. I pushed through the door moments later and came face to face with my father.

"I heard your fiancée paid you a visit," he said, amusement dancing in his tone.

My father wasn't exactly a man who found things openly amusing, so to see the sparkle in his eyes at the mention of Lucia annoyed me.

"Glad to see you're still with us."

I ignored what was now becoming a running joke and maneuvered around his large body. The man had four inches on my six-foot-two frame and about ninety extra pounds on top of that.

"She pulled a gun on Brandon," I said, walking over to the security elevator and hitting the call button that doubled for a thumb scanner. "Be glad he's still here. She's a wildcard."

A wildcard that I wanted more time to play with—to bend to my will. She'd played that sweet role with a gun strapped to her and that turned me on more than it should have. She was smart, knowing when to be cool and demure, but her feelings about my *zio* were clear to me. His dismissal of her was his first mistake, and because I knew my uncle, it wouldn't be his last.

My father hummed and followed me inside once the doors opened, Malik being the last to enter.

"He's flexing his position," he said, leaning against the wall. "Wanting to see how much power he still has over us. We still have something he'd like to utilize."

I glanced at the man who raised me, taking in his relaxed features. He believed in the process, taking one step at a time without showing your hand too soon but, more importantly, never too late. I wanted to make him proud—I wanted to show him that I was meant to take his place when the time came.

Growing up, I'd thought I was being groomed to be head of the Bianchi empire, and in a way, I still was. Just not the one I'd been preparing for. Starting over felt like a slap to the face, but my father never once blinked an eye at the blatant disrespect from our *famiglia*.

"Let it go."

His eyes met mine.

"A vengeful man never truly gets what he wants, and if by some miracle he does, its glory only lasts a short while. But a man who moves smart, with his head on straight and eyes clear of all haze, will always come out on top."

The elevator doors opened into the casino's security suite, and we all exited. Malik walked over to the multiple monitors where he kept the systems updated, and we went straight for the wall of television screens that showed real-time footage of every angle of the casino, including outside and in the parking garages.

I eyed each screen, taking in the crowded floor while allowing his words to work their way through me. It was easier said than done, but the shift in the weight of power in the mafia was necessary.

"Attack the business, never the man," I said more so to myself.

"Chop the head off and watch the empire fall."

Contrary to belief, the head was never the man at the top himself; the connections, money, and the bottom line kept the men loyal to the Don—or boss. When the money dried up, chaos ensued within the family. Once your *famiglia* was in disarray, the rest was history.

In this instance, we'd be upsetting more than one syndicate. Lucia's family background wasn't pretty, and when the Costas learned that their discarded heir was undoubtedly tying his family to mine, it would only ignite the already slow-burning flame.

"For now, we need to keep the peace," I said. "Are there any leads on Pietro's shooter?"

"There are murmurs about it possibly being one of the Reds," he replied, swiping his finger over one of the screens to change its angle.

"In other words, nothing."

Blaming the Reds was the usual line of defense when no one had any tangible answers. Using an organization with faceless assassins as an excuse was a cop-out, to say the least.

"Any info on why my staff is being targeted?"

"I have someone on it," was all he offered.

The sudden secrecy meant he had an idea but wouldn't share it until he was certain. That could take time, and time wasn't on my side with me marrying Lucia in only a few short days. Having the Costas poking around my place of business would put her at risk.

"We need all forms of identification scanned," I called to Malik. "No more simple glances at the birthdate for entry. Everyone coming through the main entrance is an enemy until I say they aren't."

"Who are you replacing Joseph with?"

"I don't know. Malik won't take the offer."

"He's dedicated to protecting your life, not anyone else's. Let your brother take care of security; for the time being, you have other responsibilities I need you focused on."

"I'm sure Matteo will enjoy that," I mumbled at the same time he came sauntering into the room with Rocco in tow.

"What will Matteo enjoy?" he asked, looking between the two of us.

"You're the new head of security until further notice."

He scoffed, and our father tossed him a look that had him straightening up immediately.

"Is that an issue, *Figlio*?"

"Not as long as I'm only meant to find Joseph's replacement."

"The faster you find one, the quicker you're off babysitting duties. I'll leave you three to it." He moved toward the door. "Let's try to keep our noses clean until after the wedding. The last thing I need is a mess to clean up."

"Sometimes I think that man hates me," Matteo said, his lips twisting.

It was meant to sound like a joke, but I heard a little truth in it, something I'd figured out about my brother a while ago. He didn't feel appreciated or seen as valuable by our father simply because he was the second-born son. And while our father was a good man, he treated us all differently. There could be a method to his madness, but I did my best to show my brother that *I* appreciated and saw his value every day, just in case.

"Gastone and Orlando will tag-team security here while we handle our other responsibilities. Brandon will do his job for once in his fucking life and fill the new position."

"Aren't they supposed to be on Lucia?" Rocco asked, his eyes scanning the monitors.

"I called them off until after the wedding..." I checked my watch and moved toward the door. "Shipment is a little late, isn't it?"

"That's why we're here," Matteo said, him and Rocco following me out. "Shipment isn't just late..."

"It never showed," Rocco finished. "I left my guys to it, but Hopper called after forty minutes and no sign of it. We were waiting on you to finish up with your guest..."

I heard the teasing note in his tone about *my* guest.

She'd been a surprise boost to my otherwise repetitive day. When Orlando said she'd instructed them to drive her here, a surge of energy burst through me—a thrill I couldn't describe but wanted to feel again.

I cut a glare in his direction.

"You should've come sooner."

"I gave him the order not to," Matteo interjected. "There's nothing you can do other than put in a few calls. For right now, we're good on supply. And if we need to source from somewhere else, I'm sure the O'Sullivans can be of assistance."

When we separated ourselves from Giovanni, we lost the endless supply of weapons they had at their disposal. I'd been able to quickly make a purchase because of Cian O'Sullivan, one of the five sons of Darragh O'Sullivan—the Irish Mob's boss. He'd strategically placed himself in the right place at the right time.

"It shouldn't come to that..." I pulled out my phone and brought up Pedro's contact. He was the go-between for the Mexican cartel leader as I was for my father. "...I'll get it sorted out."

We continued down into the basement, taking the first left into a large working space outside the tunnel that stretched a mile long and opened up to a secluded private road. It had been the reason Matteo, and I invested in the building after the casino opened. Having our own way to get anything in and out of New Jersey without being spotted gave us the upper hand. Something our uncle still wanted access to.

"Enzo, my friend," Pedro spoke after I drifted away from Matteo and Rocco and dialed him. "To what do I owe this call?"

He didn't sound like he knew his men hadn't shown.

"Is there a reason why my shipment is delayed?"

Pedro didn't respond right away, and then a long sigh filled the line.

"I took your uncle to be a man of his word," he said, his already thick accent even harder to understand through his anger. "He went to Manuel."

He wouldn't say more, but there was no need for it. I ended the call and turned to Matteo.

"Gio got to Manuel," I told him. "Set up a meeting with Cian. It's time we start using the resources the Delegation offers us."

"What are we going to do about Gio?'

"Let him play his hand until he has nothing left."

"Do nothing..." he took out his phone. "Got it."

We didn't have a say in what happened to our uncle in the end, but we knew what we were tasked to do by our father.

Keep your head up, eyes open, and move accordingly.

I'd already veered once from that path; it couldn't happen again.

Chapter 5

Lucia

"You only have twenty minutes," Gaia drawled through the earpiece I was wearing.

I removed my Glock from the holster around my waist and pushed open the door at the bottom of the stairwell leading into the basement at my parents' estate.

"I only need ten."

All movement stopped when I entered.

A few of my father's men moved to allow me through while also giving me a view of the face I went to great lengths to find in the short window of opportunity given to me.

"Do you know who I am?" I asked, coming to a stop in front of my guest.

Mariana Costa lifted her gaze, blood pooling from the wound in her temple.

She stared directly into my eyes but didn't speak. And maybe the duct tape on her mouth was the reason, but I had a feeling it wasn't.

Mariana had done what I liked to call an ultimate act of

betrayal from someone within the mafia ranks. Only, she wasn't a part of just anyone's mafia; she was a part of the one that discarded my father and late grandmother without a care in the world.

We shared DNA, but she wasn't family.

She was an enemy to my *almost* new family and guilty by association from the last name alone. Mariana was the perfect wedding present.

"To my family, I'm Luci," I went on, circling her chair. "But outside of this estate, I'm Scarlet."

I smirked when she flinched against her restraints.

"Oh..." I moved to stand in front of her again. "You recognize the nickname?"

Her eyes were large, and I chuckled.

"Let me ask you something..." I kneeled in front of her and ripped the duct tape from her mouth. "What was it like growing up?"

"You're a disgrace," she spewed.

I hummed and tipped my head to the side.

"Oh yeah? Go ahead and elaborate on that for me. I love a good story."

"I'm not a fucking jester."

I connected the butt of my gun with her cheek two times before stepping back and admiring my handy work. Mariana's fair and easily bruised skin rapidly changed to a dark shade of purple, my favorite.

"No, but I could make you one. Maybe all the families here to see me get married will enjoy the show. I'm sure the groom would be elated."

She'd not only put herself on the line, but she'd gone against the code. Fucking with another man's business was a death sentence in the mafia. The Costas were well aware of that, yet here goes their precious pawn.

"I did what I had to for my family," she said, spitting blood from her mouth. "I see you're doing the same."

"I feel sorry for you," I told her, running the barrel of my gun down my arm. The steel had a warmth to it that I enjoyed; it calmed me. "You've been trying to prove yourself to them for how long? All your life? What's it like wanting to be seen as more than just a woman? I wouldn't know. My father..." I paused. "You know him, right? Leonardo Moretti?" She blinked in response, but I saw the flare of recognition. "Don't worry about answering; everyone knows him. He never clipped my wings, and now here we are. I'm the one with the gun, and you're tied to a chair while your family is scrambling to find out who shot their heir. I just have one question for you... do you think they know you're missing?"

"It doesn't matter. I did what was needed."

"I hate to break it to you, but you're dying without having accomplished what you were sent to do."

"Are you sure about that?"

I smiled at the confidence in her voice.

"Well..." I shrugged and walked forward again, pushing her head up with the barrel of my Glock. "You said you did it for your family, but they'll all be meeting you soon. I wonder how Pietro's shoulder is doing?"

I watched as the realization of what my words meant sunk in.

"It feels good to be a Moretti. Can you imagine the whispers? A Costa woman by blood but a Moretti by honor slaughtered an entire mafia family with a smile on her face. I hope they let you watch in hell. It'll be a good show."

The corners of my lips lifted higher as she struggled against her restraints.

"I have a secret I want to share but you have to promise to take it to the grave."

I laughed, finding my joke pretty funny, and then leaned down to whisper something only she would know. When I stood straight again, I smiled wide.

"Fuck you," she screamed, rearing her head back in an attempt to headbutt me. "Kill me and get it over with."

I wrapped my free hand around her throat before she could connect and gripped it tight.

"No, Mariana..." I continued to squeeze, enjoying the defeat in her gaze. "Fuck you and with pleasure."

I released her and stood tall, backing away just far enough to give her hope.

"Enzo sends his love."

I lifted my gun and pulled the trigger, emptying my clip into her for good measure.

"Take this," I ordered, handing my useless handgun over and taking one filled with ammo from my guard. "Drop her body off on Costa territory."

I left the basement and returned to my makeshift bridal suite, where Gaia, Jaz, and Violet were waiting. I pulled my earpiece out and handed it to Gaia.

"Less than fifteen minutes," Jaz mused, fidgeting with the dress she was in. "You're getting better."

I smiled and sat in front of the vanity where my makeup artist had set up her things.

"Does Luca know?" Violet asked, her voice just above a whisper.

I watched her move around the room through the mirror before responding.

"He will eventually..."

She met my gaze and nodded.

My brother wouldn't be happy that I'd taken it upon myself to kill on our grounds without the consent of him or my father.

And because Violet liked to keep the peace, she was preparing for when he did find out.

"Look what I have for you."

Gaia slapped a manila envelope down on the vanity with a bright smile on her face.

"What is it?" I asked, not in the least bit interested.

My cousin got excited about many things, and most of them weren't up my alley of fun or gift-worthiness. She was a lover of fine electronics and into all things technology, especially when it meant she could dig into someone's life.

"Information on your soon-to-be husband."

Ah.

Her excitement made even more sense now.

"I don't need it."

I caught the tail end of a frown just before closing my eyes and allowing the makeup artist to perfect my signature winged eyeliner.

I could almost hear the pout in her voice when she asked, "But why not? It's bad enough that this marriage is arranged but having to do this without knowing more than what's being said in quiet whispers is absurd."

It was absurd, but there was more to it than even Gaia could ever understand.

"I told you she wouldn't want to see it," Violet said softly.

"I also told you the same," Jaz cosigned.

"Yeah, well, the way I see it—"

Voices outside of the door stopped her from continuing, and then my mother entered next, her voice slightly gone from all the talking she'd been doing to prepare for this wedding.

"How much longer?" she asked, the scent of her favorite perfume closer than it had been before. "She should've been out of this chair thirty minutes ago."

"It's a simple look," the artist replied. "I'll be done in five minutes."

"Mom…" I opened my eyes and found an identical pair staring back at me. "Relax."

She blew out a frustrated breath and glanced around the room.

"At least you three are ready."

"I was the first to be done, auntie," Gaia said, an innocent smile on her face.

"Mmhm," she hummed, fluffing one of Gaia's curls before returning her gaze to mine. "Give us the room."

I sighed and nodded when the makeup artist looked at me through the mirror.

"I thought you wanted me ready."

"I want to know why your father's men were guarding the basement door with their lives an hour ago, and now they're nowhere to be found?"

"I sent them away…" I waved my hand around. "They weren't needed there anymore."

"On your wedding day?" she questioned, clearly exasperated with my *extracurricular activities*.

"Business is business no matter the day."

She rolled her eyes but smiled right after.

My mother grew up on the south side of Chicago, away from the life we live now. Her parents were school teachers and upstanding citizens. They knew nothing of what being attached to the mafia was like. That being said, my mother's lack of experience hadn't stopped her from loving my father fiercely and then following him to Pennsylvania.

"You let that Italian fool turn you into something we don't respect."

I'd heard my grandmother say when my mother took us to Chicago to see her and our grandfather for the first time.

That Italian fool was my father.

He was also Black, but they'd made sure not to include that in their insults.

"Besides," I went on, standing to finish my own makeup. "This particular situation was the perfect gift for my groom."

"Lucia Moretti, if this gift comes with blood on any part of my land, I'll have your head."

I grinned at the threat.

She was cute when serious but also slightly deadly after being married to my father for so long. His ways had rubbed off on her.

"No blood involved from this point on." I glanced at her through the mirror. "I promise."

She narrowed her eyes but ultimately took my word for it and nodded.

"Let's get you in this God-forsaken dress before your father appears."

My lips curled as she unzipped the garment bag, revealing the dress I'd picked, much to her dismay.

It was red—mermaid style, one shoulder with a long sleeve—and dripped in Swarovski crystals. The dress had been sitting on display in the Baker's Clothing Bar window in downtown Philadelphia. When I'd laid eyes on it, there wasn't a single person on this planet—including my mother—who could stop me from getting it.

"You don't think he'll love it?' I asked, faux innocent.

"Not the time for your mess, Lucia," she grumbled. "Get those girls back in here to help me with this thing."

I did as I was told, and within fifteen minutes, they had me secured in my dress.

"Well, shit," Gaia murmured, her eyes wide.

I looked down at myself and then around the room to find everyone with similar expressions. Each of them had seen me in it already, but it was almost as if it were the first time again.

"This is me taking back what I said," my mother began, stepping in front of me. "I think this might be your color."

"They don't call her Scarlet for nothing," Jaz blurted.

Violet nodded, and I spun around to look into the full-length mirror.

Mmm.

Maybe red was my color.

A knock at the door and then an invitation from my mother for our guest to enter produced my father and brother.

Luca smirked at my choice of dress.

On the other hand, my father didn't seem amused by it.

"Lucia..."

"Don't get her started, Leonardo," my mother interjected, moving to stand beside him. "You encouraged her to be the woman she is today, save the traditional talk for never."

"Do me a favor, *Figlia.*" Daughter. "Try not to kill the man before sun up?"

My lips curved immediately, and he chuckled.

My father hadn't said it aloud, but I knew he loved the fire I had inside of me. I'd learned it from him first. He led our family with grace and an iron fist. I loved him as the man who helped raise me, but I respected him even more as the head of our *famiglia.*

"That's a promise I can keep."

He nodded, and Luca stepped forward, taking one of my hands in his before leaning to whisper in my ear.

"I know you can handle yourself," he said. "And there isn't a doubt in my mind that ole boy has his work cut out for him, but if you ever need an out..." I pulled back to look him in the eyes, and he shook his head, silencing what he knew was coming next. "...if you ever need an out, come to me, Luci. Come to me, and I'll get you out."

I squeezed his hands and nodded.

My brother had voiced his disdain for arranged marriages on more occasions than I could account for.

"Always and forever, right?"

"Emphasis on forever. I'll light the entire tri-state on fire for you."

The declaration wasn't new. We'd been saying it since I could remember, but it felt more significant this time—like the beginning of something neither of us could see coming.

"Emphasis on forever," I repeated softly before he stepped away and left the room with everyone following behind him besides our father.

"Are you ready? There's no turning back once we leave this room."

I took a deep breath and flipped my red lace veil over my face.

"I'm ready," I declared, slipping my arm through his.

The real question was, *is my soon-to-be husband ready for me?*

Chapter 6

Enzo

"You haven't seen your *Nonna* in a while." I looked down at my mother as she adjusted my tie for the fifth time. She'd taken the opportunity to catch me while I was alone. Our conversations tended to go better without listening ears and multiple strong, opinionated personalities joining in.

She was nervous about a lot, and rightfully so with the way our lives had changed over the last six months. When Emilia Bianchi got nervous, she took joy in fixing everything in sight. It didn't matter that I'd fixed my tie to perfection; she found an issue and went to town, knowing I wouldn't do a thing to stop her.

"I know."

She lifted her gaze and frowned.

"You're purposely not seeing her?"

"I—"

"Enzo, I know you're having a hard time adjusting to the changes we've endured." She smoothed the silk with her fingers and then dropped her hands. "I get it, but she's your grandmother, and she lost her husband. She lost her son, too."

She didn't *lose* a son.

He was pushed out and did what was best for him, for *us*.

How was I supposed to tell my mother that the woman she was standing up for, who I admittedly loved dearly, refused to see any of us? Even the son she *lost*?

The businessman in me understood why it would look bad, why she'd chosen sides more or less, but deep down, where my inner child lived, I had feelings about it. Shit I would never admit aloud.

My father hadn't told my mother because she was an empath, naturally soft-spoken, and easily affected by chaos or someone else's pain. She connected with everyone, and every day he did his due diligence to protect her from emotional harm. Her heart was bigger than life, and there were moments when I wondered how she managed to stomach the life we lived.

"You've seen her?" I asked instead.

"We had a conversation," she admitted, her voice just above a whisper.

"I wish I could say it was me..." I picked up the jacket to my tux and slipped it on. "...but right now, things are complicated with Giovanni."

Giovanni was making things complicated. I believed in stooping to another man's level to prove a point, and my *Zio* needed a reality check. But, timing was important.

"Remember, family is everything."

I lifted my gaze to meet hers.

"I'm not the one who needs to be reminded about family, and from where I'm standing, all the family I need hasn't abandoned me."

"Enzo—"

"I'm getting married," I cut in. "Tell me what I'm supposed to do about that, and we can discuss anything you want another day."

One perfectly arched brow rose.

"Are you asking me for advice?"

I turned away from her assessing gaze and picked up my Glock to secure it on my person. The idea that asking for advice on how to deal with a marriage like the one I was entering meant more than it was supposed to made me feel easy to read.

"She has a look in her eyes," she said after moments of silence. "It's not all dark in there, and maybe the right person can bring it out of her."

I picked up my watch and considered her words.

"I'm not meant to be the man who does that."

"So another man is?"

An emotion I refused to decipher rushed to the forefront of my mind; I closed my eyes and released a deep breath.

"Another man while she's attached to me?" I asked, returning to fastening my watch around my wrist.

"She'll only ever be attached to you, Enzo," she responded. "Alliance arranged or not, Lucia will be your wife. You can be all of what's expected of you and *more*."

I schooled my features and turned.

"Any more advice for me?"

"That anger inside of you isn't worth what will come from it."

Tired of hearing about the anger I was harboring, I nodded and checked the time.

"Where's Matteo and—"

The door to the room we'd been loaned by Lucia's mother opened, and Matteo appeared first with Gianna hot on his heels.

"Are you ready?" he asked, looking me over and then turning to our mother. "Did you tell him not to provoke his bride?"

She smiled and slipped her arm through his.

"I told him what needed to be heard."

"You've mastered pretending like the rest of us; I'm sure your marriage will be fruitful," Gianna offered before turning and leaving the room.

"Fuck is her problem?"

"When doesn't she have a problem?" Matteo mused, unbothered by our sister. "Deal with it tomorrow. Tonight we drink."

"Be on your best behavior, Matteo Bianchi."

He grinned down at her.

"Anything for you, Ma."

Matteo pulled her out of the room—but tossed a knowing look in my direction that for once I appreciated—before they completely disappeared. I needed a minute to breathe alone without interruption.

Shaking my head, I walked over to the makeshift bar they'd added for me. Though I'd never been much of a drinker, I poured two fingers of bourbon into the glass tumbler and knocked it back.

After pouring one more for good measure, I peered around the room. My gaze lingered on the bookcase, and I moved toward it after setting my glass down. The books weren't real, not like the collection in their library. It made me wonder what was hiding behind it, but I didn't have time to inspect it.

"Bossman," Rocco greeted, knocking and then letting himself in. "I was asked to give you this."

He handed me a white envelope with my name scrawled in red across it.

To my soon-to-be husband, I told you I didn't take kindly to people fucking with my family. You're my family now, so I thought I'd give you something to show what I meant by that. I took it upon myself to take care of a little problem for you as a wedding gift. Tell your security they shouldn't talk so openly for others to hear."

I flipped what I realized was a photo and stared at the dead girl tied to a chair. I'd never seen her up close before—she'd always worn a hat low on her face when near cameras—but I knew almost immediately that it was Mariana Costa.

This woman.

I stared at the picture a little longer and then handed it and the envelope to Rocco.

"Get rid of that when you get the chance. Let's go."

Lucia was proving to be an asset.

"It's about that time," Matteo called from the end of the hall just as Rocco and I exited the room. "Are you ready?"

Was I?

"Yeah," I said, choosing the most logical answer.

Ready or not, I was leaving Blackthorne, Pennsylvania as a married man. And when we made it out into the gardens where the ceremony was taking place, something shifted inside of me. I stood at the end of the aisle with the eyes of nearly an entire criminal underworld on me.

"Please rise for the bride," the priest spoke.

The music started—deep cords with dark undertones filled the air, and the anticipation grew as the guests stood and turned, focusing their attention in the direction she'd be coming from.

"She's..."

Matteo's voice—though I knew he was still speaking—faded when I placed eyes on Lucia being escorted to me by her father. She was draped in red, from the veil on her face down to the gown molded to her frame. Even if I'd tried, I couldn't take my eyes away.

I followed their movements until Leonardo and Lucia were standing close enough for me to reach out and take her hand.

They stalled, the music stopped, and the priest began to speak.

"Please be seated..." he paused and then continued. "Friends, family, and loved ones, we come together today, in the sight of the divine and of you as witnesses, to join Enzo Bianchi and Lucia Moretti in marriage. We gather around them now in this wonderful place, and we look on with love and hope as these two begin their new life together as one."

I kept my eyes on Lucia, and I knew she was looking back at me; I felt the intensity emanating from behind her veil. Because I wasn't feeling much like my usual patient self, I closed the small distance between us, ignoring the priest and the death glare from her father.

Not a soul in this room was going to stop me from doing what the fuck I wanted.

"Can I lift it?" I asked, staring down at her.

She removed her arm from her father's and lifted the veil herself.

Dark, overly lined eyes stared up at me—through me. Her lips were painted the same color as her dress, the rest of her makeup minimal, if I had to guess. She was fucking gorgeous.

"Did you get my gift?" she asked, her tone soft but gaze fierce.

"I did, and now I'll have to repay you."

"Mmm," she hummed, her lips curving. "There's something magical about having a man indebted to me."

My lips twitched, but I refused to openly react. Instead, I held my hand out.

"Shall we?"

She placed her palm into mine, and I led us to the makeshift altar. I released her after we faced one another and nodded for Father Mancini to continue. Our gazes never left the other, and I knew right then that I was not ready for the likes of Lucia Moretti.

Chapter 7

Lucia

There was a brief moment where I got to steal a peek at the man I would now have to share my life with from this day forward. Enzo stood tall—the only way a man of his six-foot-four stature should—with his back and shoulders straight, confidence oozing through. I let my gaze fall, noting his ruby-encrusted cufflinks peeking from under his tux jacket.

They matched the color of his tie and paired well with my dress.

That hadn't been planned.

Feeling his subtle shift in attention, I lifted my gaze and met his brown eyes. They reminded me of ground cinnamon today, making them harder to look away from.

He ran his fingers over his freshly groomed beard and licked his bottom lip before asking, "Like what you see?"

I fought not to smile.

"I see a lot of things I like, but that's neither here nor there," I said, lifting one shoulder in a lazy shrug.

Enzo's lips twitched, and then he turned away just as his uncle stepped in front of us.

"Enzo," Giovanni spoke with his gaze on me.

The disgust he wore on his face, after eyeing me up and down, brought a smile to mine. My dress made traditionalists like him upset, and I enjoyed the idea of that way too much.

Enzo's expression, on the other hand, had gone from intrigued to bored in a matter of seconds. He grabbed my hand with his, tangling our fingers together after his uncle reached out to take mine.

"Giovanni," Enzo returned. "Let me *formally* introduce you to my wife Lucia."

"We need to talk, and it needs to be sooner rather than later."

"Remember where you are, *Zio*," Enzo said, tightening his hold on my hand. "Have a drink and pretend like you want to be here. Maybe I'll make myself available to you after this is all said and done."

"You be sure to do that," Giovanni said as he walked away.

"I could kill him now, and no one would care," I mumbled, removing my hand from Enzo's.

"No one *here* would care," he corrected, taking my hand back.

I bit the inside of my cheek and fought not to snatch it away in front of our guests.

The mafia was all about politics. As much as they hated the men who stood in front of the world spewing their bullshit about making a change, they were a lot like those men, following a handbook created by a bunch of white supremacists who weren't even alive anymore.

Fuck that.

I didn't have a handbook to follow.

I made my own rules, and Giovanni Bianchi deserved a

bullet to the shoulder, maybe even between the eyes. Not being able to do that made me angry. No, it infuriated me.

"May I dance with your bride?"

"I don't know, Joaquin," Enzo said, grazing the backside of my hand over and over. "She's a little angry right now."

Ignoring Enzo, I stared at the man who'd recruited me into the Society. Joaquin had been my guard most of my life, and then one day, he disappeared. My father refused to answer my questions, and I went three years without them. Until he showed up on my seventeenth birthday and told me something that changed my life forever.

I was still angry with him.

He never explained why he left, but I figured it all out on my own.

Ten years later and my feelings were *still* hurt.

"How's your wife?" I asked, cutting my eyes to Mio Sāto.

She hadn't approached, but I felt her gaze on us. I didn't have anything against the Oyabon. There was no reason to be angry at her for her husband's actions.

"She could come speak," Enzo interjected, tightening his hold on mine.

"She doesn't want to rock the boat."

"There isn't a boat to rock..." I removed my hand from Enzo's and took Joaquin's. "One dance."

He nodded, and we moved to the dance floor my mother somehow had built in a week. But when you had money and connections, anything was possible. I cut my gaze over my shoulder to where Enzo had been standing, finding that his eyes were trained on us.

"He isn't your typical mafioso," Joaquin said, stealing my attention away from Enzo.

I placed my hands on his shoulders, and we rocked to a classic Tamia song.

"I'm not your typical mafioso princess," I quipped, staring him in the eyes.

He chuckled and nodded.

"These things, I know, Luci. But *you* need to understand that Enzo is exactly what the mafia fears. It was your dad some decades back, but he built his own without touching theirs. Enzo is taking what he learned from them and applying it to his methods. What comes down on him will ultimately come down on you."

"Is there a reason you're telling me this? I don't fear the wrath of the mafia."

I didn't fear anyone or anything. Not the mafia. Not the Society. And not Enzo Bianchi.

"I'm giving you a heads up to watch your back."

"Mmm," I hummed, staring over his shoulder at my brother as he approached from across the yard. "Sounds like you're making up for not doing the same fourteen years ago."

I released him and stepped back.

"I'm a big girl now. I can handle my own, Joaquin. But send the wife and Akira my love."

I took my brother's outstretched hand and walked into his embrace.

"What did he want?" Luca asked.

I glanced over my shoulder and said, "To warn me," before turning back.

Only it hadn't been a real warning.

Just a man realizing that he had an impact on my life at one point and fucked it up. Nothing but a man who wanted to right a wrong I wasn't ready to right yet. Maybe I was being a little hard on Joaquin. He had a job to do, and now that I was in his shoes, I understood. But it didn't make the feeling of betrayal go away.

"Warn you about what?"

"About me, if I had to guess," Enzo interjected.

Luca's features hardened, his eyes taking on a dark look I hadn't seen before. But I couldn't deal with his hate for my husband at the moment, so I turned toward Enzo.

"We need to have a little talk, Mrs. Bianchi." He glanced at Luca dismissively. "Excuse us."

He took my hand before I could reply or even come to grips with hearing my new last name. Enzo pulled me through the backyard and into the house, his long strides determined.

He twisted the knob on the first door we came upon—the library—and closed us inside. I immediately pulled my hand from his and released a deep breath. I walked over to the table in the middle of the room and opened every drawer until I found the bottle of hand sanitizer I'd left lying around.

His touch unnerved me.

I could still feel the warmth of his fingers against mine.

"So, I was right about you needing a break," Enzo said after a few moments of silence.

I poured the lavender-scented sanitizer into my hands and then gave him my attention.

"What gave it away?"

"Something about the look on your face when dancing with Joaquin. Should I be aware of something?"

"Maybe," I admitted. "Joaquin was my longtime guard until he wasn't. He's the reason I have this."

I lifted my makeup-covered wrist, and he hummed while walking the perimeter of the room. I watched him eye books along the way, stopping to pull one or two out before continuing on. Eventually, I couldn't follow him anymore because that meant turning around, which I refused to do.

I could feel him closing the distance right up until his breath was a small whisper against my neck. Close enough to make contact but enough space that we weren't touching. He was purposely straddling the line between our respective personal spaces.

I stood quietly rooted in place, waiting for him to say something.

"You wore the perfume," he said, brushing his nose up against my neck and awakening a primal side of me. "I like when you listen, *Bellissima*."

"Enzo..."

He spun me around and wrapped his fingers around my neck. His lips curved into a taunting smile, the same as they had the first time he'd gotten me like this.

"Are we not pretending anymore?" I asked, pressing my hands against his chest.

"How can I pretend when you're dripping in red, Scarlet?"

"Because we agreed to go all in."

He stared down at me with a look in his eyes that drove me fucking wild. I twisted in his hold, but he only tightened his fingers around my neck to keep me in place.

"We did," he mused, brushing his lips against mine. "But now you're a Bianchi, just like I wanted. I'm done pretending like I haven't had you before, Scarlet."

I closed my eyes, willing myself to let go of the act.

"I missed you," I whispered.

They say absence makes the heart grow fonder, and two months of not seeing his face proved that to be true. Only, I still didn't know him well enough for my heart to be so invested.

"Look at me and say it again."

I released a breath and did as he asked.

"I missed you, Enzo."

"Good..." he pulled my bottom lip into his mouth and sucked, not caring about my lipstick. "Because I missed you, too."

His lips on mine made the world fall away. His lips on

mine were becoming my kryptonite. Enzo was so much more than just being next in line to lead his family. And no one would ever be able to see that side of him because it was mine to have and protect.

"We should get back to our guests."

"Or we could leave them here and start the best part of all this a little early."

"Not a part of the plan, Enzo."

I pushed him away, and he let me, putting some distance between us.

"The plan..." his lips curved in annoyance as he walked toward the door. "We better get back to it, Lucia Bianchi."

I pulled my lips in to keep from smiling and turned to follow him out.

"Ready?" he asked after I slipped my arm through his.

"Always..."

He reached out to wipe my lips.

"Now you're ready."

I'd never been so enamored by a man before.

Until, I met *the* Enzo Bianchi.

Chapter 8

Enzo

Nine months prior

"Which one?"

Joseph pointed to the camera feed over the roulette table, right at the back of the head full of wild curls. I watched her play a few rounds, winning big but sliding her chips to the two people sitting at her right and left.

I lifted an eyebrow and cut my eyes at my head of security.

"What exactly is the problem?"

I knew what he would say, but I asked anyway, allowing him to indulge me.

"She's been here three times this week," he informed me. "Alone. Sometimes she plays. Other times she just watches."

I turned back to the screen just as she lifted her head and stared directly into the camera. Her lips curved—almost as if she knew someone was watching—and then she looked away, placed her last chip on the roulette table, and stood.

"Her name?" I asked as she pushed through a door that was off-limits to anyone not employed by my casino.

The only door that wasn't secured with a fingerprint scanner.

"Lucia Moretti."

Mmmm.

"Stay here."

I left without another word and took the stairs down to the level she'd been on. She stood at the bottom of the staircase; the scent of her perfume gave me pause. And as if she'd known I was having a moment, her lips rounded into a smirk.

"You know," she started, her tone sultry. "I thought you'd be taller."

I tipped my head at her, and she did the same.

There was a look in her eyes that said let this play out, so I leaned my body into the railing and pulled at my beard.

"I take it you know who I am..."

"Enzo Bianchi..." she crossed her arms and rested against the wall. "Your father is Angelo. Your brother is Matteo, and your sister is Gianna."

"You forgot someone."

She smiled and pushed off the wall to stand in front of me.

"I figured you'd say that, but mothers are sacred."

"And my sister isn't?"

"Your sister is not at all who you think she is."

I lifted an eyebrow, my hackles rising about why she was really here.

What would Leonardo Moretti's daughter be doing in Grayfall of all places? At my casino? Dressed in... I eyed her up and down, taking in her black cargo pants, long-sleeved black shirt, and black Timbs.

"What can I do for you, Ms. Moretti?"

Her dark eyes flared at my use of her surname before she schooled her features again.

"Has anyone ever told you that your voice vibrates through them when you speak?"

"What can I do for you, Ms. Moretti?" I asked again.

She moved in closer, her body pressing up against mine and perfume wafting my nasal cavity. Lucia smelled like something floral like she'd rolled in a field of flowers before coming here.

I flared my nostrils to take in more.

Or maybe it was lavender.

"There are a few things you can do for me, but I'd rather not talk about it in this stairwell."

I licked my lips and angled my head down to stare at her.

"And why should I trust a woman I've never encountered in person before dressed in black with a..." I tapped the Glock she had tucked in her pants behind her back. "...beautiful piece of steel on her person? I'd love to know how you got that past security, too."

"Oh, Enzo," she mused, grazing my beard with her fingers. "If I wanted you dead, you'd never have seen me coming. And if you must know, I'm resourceful. I can get my weapons into any place I want them in."

"Are you sure about that?" I asked, grabbing her fingers and pushing them away.

"I've never been so sure about something in my life." She spun around and looked over her shoulder at me. "Now, can we go talk? I have something I'd like to discuss that I think you'll want to hear."

She kept her back to me, staring at the door that only my fingerprints could get us through.

"Mind opening this?"

I moved in behind her, pressing up against her backside. A little too close for comfort based on the way her frame stilled. I reached around to tap the door handle with my thumb.

"If you want to talk…" The door clicked, and I nudged it open before it could lock again. "Then, let's go talk."

She sauntered through the opening, her hips seductively swinging from left to right. I stood back for a moment, mesmerized by what I had a feeling was her natural stride. There was nothing manufactured about it.

"Are you going to stand there staring at my back…" she gazed at me over her shoulder. "…or do you plan to show me the way?"

"Last door on the left," I said, striding forward and past her to lead the way.

I grabbed ahold of my office door and held it open, flicking my free hand as a signal for her to enter. She paused before doing so, those sultry eyes staring into mine for any sign not to trust me. If Lucia had known what was good for her, she wouldn't have shown up here at all, but now that she had, there was no turning back.

"Don't be shy now."

She scoffed and brushed past me.

"Calling me shy is an insult."

"You don't sound insulted," I mused, stepping in behind her and closing the door.

My office wasn't anything to write home about. It had a desk and a chair, and one monitor that showed feed from outside of the casino.

"Well, this is sad," she said, ignoring my assumption and falling into the only chair the room had. "What kind of office is this?"

"One that doesn't matter. We won't be here long." I crossed my arms and lifted an eyebrow. "Now talk."

"So demanding…" she spun around in the chair twice and then stopped it. "I heard about you and your family."

I didn't react or respond.

People knew what we wanted them to. This led me to believe that Lucia was fishing for more than she could find out on her own.

"We are a lot alike, you and I," she went on, twirling in the chair again. "Our fathers were never going to be accepted." She paused her childish pursuit and pinned her dark irises on me. "The only difference is yours figured it out late in life. Mine was never allowed the opportunity to know his true family."

There was a hint of anger in her cadence.

She didn't try hiding it, and I found that to be intriguing.

I found *her* intriguing.

Lucia was stunningly gorgeous. Enough that I couldn't keep my eyes off her every move.

I noticed it all.

The subtle shift in her arms. Or the way she lifted one eyebrow and her lips curved as she spoke, almost as if she were smiling, but really it was a tactic to hold back.

Ms. Moretti had a lot of secrets.

"And you want what? Revenge?" I asked, tone dry—bored.

That awarded me a glare and flicker of annoyance from the princess. She sat up straight and pressed her hands into the wooden desktop, her gaze flittering over to the screen in front of her and then back at me.

"I heard you were a man with morals, Bianchi. That you still believe in leaving women and children out of our business. Is that true, or have I made a mistake in coming here?"

The assumptions were true.

I preferred to keep mafioso business *in* the mafia.

But instead of repeating my thoughts aloud, I shrugged.

My nonchalant reply angered her. The fire that had slowly risen in her eyes ignited bright red with an orange hue. The sight of it made my dick hard.

"Depends on why you came here."

"The Costas are deep into the skin trade," she revealed, the fire dulling a bit. "It started off small. Unnoticeable. And then it turned into three girls a week. Every month there's more. I can't save them all."

I stared at her, fighting the urge to take a step forward. There was an inflection in her tone that gave me the urge to protect. From what? I had no fucking clue, and that alone was disturbing.

"And you came here for what?" I lifted an eyebrow. "My help?"

She shook her head and stood, walking around the desk and then coming to a stop in front of me.

"I came with a proposition."

I dropped my gaze and slowly perused her frame from the tips of her boots, over the curve of her hips, and the swell of her breasts.

"What exactly…" I brought my gaze to meet hers. "…can you do for me, Ms. Moretti?"

"Bianchi…" she scrutinized me the same as I'd done her, pulling her bottom lip between her teeth. "There are so many things that I can *do* for you…" her gaze met mine again, that fire was replaced with lust. "…but I'm not here to act on the sexual tension in the room. I'm here to offer your father a place in The Delegation."

That got *my* attention.

"What makes you think my father cares to have a seat at your father's table?"

"Your father might not but *you*…" She smiled, her heart-shaped lips curving and spreading in a way that made my dick twitch. "Enzo Bianchi, next in line to lead his *new* family, has a plan that could work faster if he had the right people at his back. The right resources."

Mmm.

The Delegation was a goal on my list to accomplish, but it wasn't as high up as she thought. I had other plans, other shit to handle and prove before making a go for it. Lucia stared at me, a smug expression on her face. Like she'd cracked the code.

Only she'd just given me a better idea.

I closed the distance between us in quick strides, backing Lucia into the desk and gripping her hair. She'd been caught off guard, something I was almost certain never happened. But it didn't take long for her to react. She raised her left hand and pulled a razor from her mouth, laying it right up against my neck.

I smiled.

This woman was an enigma, and I wanted a piece of her—every melanated inch.

"Has anyone ever told you how sexy it is that you carry a blade in your mouth?"

With her chest heaving against mine, she pricked my skin, and I hissed, feeling a small amount of blood trickle down my neck.

"Mmm," she hummed, her lips lifting as I tightened my hold on her hair, tugging her head back to expose her slender neck. "Someone likes a little knife play."

"What do you need?" I asked up against the shell of her ear, brushing my erection up the side of her thigh. "From me, that is."

"Under the building next door, there's a tunnel." She dropped her hand, and I released her hair, wiping the blood away from my skin. "I don't care what you use it for; I need it."

I rubbed my fingers together, smearing the blood into my skin before looking at her again.

"I need something in return."

"The Del—"

"Not the Delegation," I cut in, running my tongue over my teeth. "I need something else."

She lifted an eyebrow and angled her head to the left, a small smile playing on her lips. Almost as if she'd seen this coming. Which only made me want her more.

"What is it that I can do for you?"

I shrugged, making what I was about to say seem like nothing when it was everything.

"You can marry me."

Lucia stilled, all the playfulness gone from her demeanor.

Marriage wasn't shit to joke about, especially when you came from families like ours.

This...

Asking her to marry me wasn't a part of my plan, and it damn sure hadn't been a part of my father's. I was making moves that could only be approved by him, but now that I'd made my mind up, not even he could stop me from doing it.

"Why the fuck would you want to marry me?" she asked, sounding offended.

I chuckled.

"Why the fuck not?" I threw back, enjoying the panicked look bouncing around in her gaze. "You want something from me that'll put my men at risk. The only way I can trust you aren't fucking me over is by a good ole fashion arranged marriage. Your initial offer isn't sufficient enough."

"I thought they said you were level-headed."

"This is as level-headed as it gets."

In the end, marrying Lucia not only linked our families together for life but the seat at the table she offered? It would ultimately belong to my father and then me.

"You must think I'm stupid?"

"I don't think anything of you," I said, deadpanned.

That angered her, and seconds later, I was staring down the barrel of her Glock.

"I could kill you with ease," she sniped as I stepped forward, allowing the slightly warmed steel to graze the skin of my forehead.

"Death is a part of life, Lucia. If it's my time to go, then so be it."

I never feared it, and I never would, not even when it's staring me in the face with red-tinted lips. Kissable lips. A mouth that would look perfect wrapped around my dick while I fucked it.

"But," I went on, sealing our fate. "If you shoot me here, I can guarantee you won't make it out alive. Then, who's going to save those girls you came here for? Hm?"

The war she was having with herself played like a series of photos flashing right before my eyes. If it hadn't been something as serious as sex trafficking, she would've pulled the trigger and tried her luck. But this cause meant something to her, and that meant she'd do anything to put a stop to it, including marrying me.

"I think Lucia Bianchi has a nice ring to it," I taunted, sidestepping her outstretched arm.

"We both know you won't shoot me. It's an ego thing at the moment, right?"

She stared up at me, her gun pointed at the door now, and hatred in her eyes.

"How about this..." I leaned forward, purposely brushing my face up against hers. "Shoot the door and let out all of that aggression," I whispered into her ears. "Or, I could fuck it out of you right now."

The sexual tension between us was thick. Her scent was driving me wild, and I could feel her draw to me. It was hard to miss. *She* was hard to fucking miss, and I wanted to keep her.

Lucia fired her gun—the sound of wood splitting from the impact—and I laughed, moving away from her as she tucked it on her person again.

"I knew you'd give me a hard time, but marriage..." she scoffed. "Fucking insane."

I ignored her and opened the door, finding Rocco on the other side with one thick brow raised in question.

"Bossman, is there a reason why this door has a bullet hole in it?"

Lucia chuckled.

"If you let me shoot him, I'll say yes."

Rocco leaned to the side to get a view of the hellion behind me, both his eyebrows lifted now. He grinned like the crazy mothafucka he was and asked, "If I let her shoot me, what is she saying yes to?"

"Marrying me."

He hummed and eyed her closely.

"Don't I know you?"

"I don't know," she mused, moving to stand beside me. "Do you?"

"She's a Moretti."

He nodded and said, "Alright then. Avoid any places on my body that'll put me out of commission for a long time."

I cut my eyes at Lucia, and she had hers on him.

"It's no fun when the other party is in agreeance."

"Then that's settled." He looked away from her to me. "You good here?"

I waved for him to go, and he moved to do just that before pausing and glancing at Lucia again, his gaze scrutinizing her frame but not in the same way that I had. It was more out of curiosity than anything, which piqued mine.

"I'm digging the look," he complimented, smirking. "You'd think you were an assassin or something."

Then, he disappeared, but the infliction in his tone had my hackles rising once more.

"Something you'd like to tell me?"

She laughed.

"No can do, *boss man*. I'll see you around." She paused at the door and glanced over her shoulder at me. "There's a meeting scheduled to take place soon. My father has an issue your father can take care of as his way in. He can propose marriage there. All *you* have to do is convince him."

"That won't be a problem."

"So you say..."

This time she moved to leave, but I stopped her by wrapping my fingers around her forearm and pulling her back.

"Have dinner with me."

She didn't turn but snatched her arm from my hold.

"Why would I do that?"

"Because there's something you need from me, remember? We need to discuss it."

She twisted to face me, revealing the look she'd been trying to hide.

Lust.

"Is it my touch or my tone that has that look in your eyes right now?"

It disappeared instantly, and I smirked.

"Find a place no one knows our names and I'll be there."

"And how will I find you?" I asked, already knowing the answer but wanting to hear her voice again.

She smiled and turned, leaving the room and me behind.

"I'm sure you'll figure it out. A man like you has the necessary resources to track a person down. Find me, and I'll even stay for a drink after I order the largest steak on the menu."

"You can do whatever you want," I said, going into the hall just to see that seductive sway she called walking.

Lucia pulled open the door we'd come through damn near an hour ago, giving me one last look before disappearing through it.

"I'll be seeing you, Ms. Moretti."

Real soon.

Chapter 9

Lucia

"I don't like this, Lucia," Gaia fumed, unloading and reloading her Glock. "We work better with the four of us. Including more people will only mess with the flow of things. Especially when *you* can't always be present."

"Gaia..."

She cut an evil glare in my direction, and I smirked.

Gaia's anger was warranted, and returning the attitude would get me nowhere in convincing her we needed the extra manpower to continue on. I hadn't banked on part of that extra manpower pulling a fast one on me.

You agreed to it!

I had no clue why I did it.

Aiming my gun at Enzo had been the only thing I could think to do to stop myself from blurting *yes* right away.

He wasn't like any man I'd ever met.

My reaction to him... *the draw*. It scared me, and I had a habit of taking on scary things for fun.

"I agree with G," Jaz chimed in from her place in front of

the security screens. "New people means possible new threats to our operation."

She flipped her braids to one side of her body and turned to look at me, pushing her glasses up on her pretty face. Jazmina Porter was Haitian American. She'd grown up in the Bronx most of her life and had an attitude to boot. The girl was only five-two at most but a fighter through and through. That first drew me to her.

I took a deep breath and turned my attention to Violet. She'd only been with us for a year after being rescued from a stolen transport in New Jersey, almost identical to the way Gaia and I had saved Jazmina just two years before that.

Violet Jackson was tall, standing over my five-foot-seven frame, and had the most beautiful dark complexion. She wore her hair in two large puffs today and was built like a supermodel, with a wiry stature and bone structure most women hired doctors to get. Her personality was the complete opposite of Jaz's. She was soft-spoken but not afraid to speak up for herself.

The real difference between the two? Jazmina buried what happened to her so deep that if you asked her about the day she was snatched off a street in New York, she wouldn't be able to answer with the complete truth. Violet, on the other hand, chose to wear her emotions on her sleeve. She chose to feel *everything* all the time. And being betrayed by a man she'd loved hadn't changed her openness.

"What about you, Vi? Are you against bringing in help?"

She took her time responding, her gaze slowly moving in my direction. Those dark grey eyes of hers met mine, and all of the stories behind them flashed.

"I think it's time," she spoke softly, wrinkling her nose. "There are more girls out there who won't get a second chance like us…" her voice trailed as she met Jaz's intense gaze. "If we can save more this way, then I'm all for it."

"She's right," Gaia grumbled. "I'll do whatever is needed."

I opened my mouth to speak, to thank them for trusting me, but the chance was stolen from me.

"Incoming," Jaz announced as a motorcycle and slate grey Range Rover pulled up in front of our safe house. "Your people?"

I nodded and picked up my gun, stashing it in the holster around my torso. Walking toward the front entry, I punched in the security code, and the steel security gate lifted, revealing a regular wood-framed door. I glanced over my shoulder briefly and then pulled it open.

"Why did you bring him?" I asked, stepping out of the house and earshot of my girls.

Monroe cut her eyes at me and then her husband, Sheldon Black. He was the head of the Black crime family in New York. Monroe was the head of the Harper crime family in Chicago. The two of them had been arranged to be married way before they were born, and now that they're together, both are the heads of the now combined Black-Harper crime family, one of the biggest crime families operating on the East Coast and Midwest. Anyone who was anyone knew that Sheldon was tamer than his wife, and right now, I needed unhinged, not tame.

"I thought you liked him," Monroe said, smiling in my direction.

Sheldon leaned his back against the front of the Range Rover and crossed his arms. The corner of his mouth was lifted into a smug smirk because he knew exactly why I didn't want him here.

"You two are easier to work with when you're not together," I told her.

"I have to agree with Scarlet," Seven said after removing her helmet and climbing off her bike. "The two of you together is frustrating, to say the least," she added.

Seven—or Prissy as most called her—was the President of the Queen of Hearts motorcycle club in Chicago—an all-Black female-only one percent club, to be exact. They were known for being allies with a few different families, but everyone knew that Seven's loyalty was to her childhood best friend, Monroe. I didn't really need Seven, but she was a part of their team. Together these three had ties deeper than any family in the underworld. Having their resources was the best possible scenario.

"Here's the problem," Sheldon said, eyes on me. "We already have enough shit going on, and if it were up to my *wife*..." he cut his eyes at her but only briefly. "She would do this no questions asked, and while I also understand the severity of your cause, we still have a family to run. I'm here to make sure that this plan you're working up does not fuck with my bottom line."

He continued to stare at me, and I held his gaze for a while before nodding. I understood where Sheldon was coming from because I, too, came from a family just like his. Compromising wasn't one of my strongest attributes, but for this cause, I would do whatever it took.

"Come inside, and let's talk."

I turned and walked back into the safe house with Sheldon, Monroe, and Seven following behind me. After everyone was inside, I punched in a different code, and the security door dropped—locking us all in.

I was appreciative that I didn't need to make any introductions. Everyone in the room had already met and was well acquainted. But personal wasn't business and I knew it would take more to convince my girls to be okay with this.

"Let me show you something," I said, walking over to the large table sitting in the middle of the room. I rolled open a map that showed every receiving dock between New York and Pennsylvania. "Every red dot you see on here are hot spots for trafficking. It's close enough to the docks that they can get them in and out of the country without much effort. We'd been able to intercept shipments before, but it's getting harder."

I stepped back and allowed them to circle the table. Sheldon's usual cool demeanor changed almost immediately. I knew a fire building inside of someone when I saw it.

"I'm not here to fuck up your bottom line," I said. "But I am here to fuck up someone else's."

Monroe lifted her head, pushing her locs back to look me directly in my eyes.

"Every one of these docks is in Costa territory. We share the same transports."

I nodded.

"We know that their territory is bordering yours," Gaia said, stepping forward. "The treaty between your families and theirs gives you access to more information than we can get alone."

"There's a treaty between the Italians in general and us," Sheldon said, lifting his thick eyebrows in my direction. "That is not only fucking with my bottom line, but it also means possibly starting a street war. I like my streets quiet. This..." He pointed to the map. "...is bigger than you're trying to make it."

"It's bigger than any of us realize. *Innocent* people are being snatched off the streets right before your eyes, and nobody seems to give a fuck but me... but *us*." I waved to my girls. "If you've witnessed what I have, you wouldn't be questioning this at all."

The truth of the matter was no one actually gave a fuck because as long as it made money, then it made sense to them. I never claimed to be a good person, nor would I ever, because I was not. But this was unacceptable, and I refused to let it ride.

"There's been chatter about them slowing up. And the media bombarding the news cycle with multiple missing person cases takes leads me to believe it's true. I just need to know if they have something big planned before going underground with it."

"You think once they disappear, the girls will be lost forever?"

I nodded.

Silence filled the space around us as Sheldon and Monroe spoke to one another with their eyes.

It was something they annoyingly did often.

I'd met Monroe during a contract I took in Chicago. A mafia princess could spot another from a mile away. If I had taken a good look at her, I would've known immediately, but she'd spotted me first. We were a lot alike, Monroe and me. If I had to consider someone my friend, she would be it.

Eventually, they turned to me, and I knew what was coming next; I had prepared for it.

"If we take this risk, then we need something in return to make up for what might possibly come," Monroe said, crossing her arms.

They would stand to lose a lot and in this world, knowingly signing yourself up to take a loss was blasphemy. It was unheard of. But, I had ties to something that I knew they wanted. The same thing I'd offered Enzo.

"If you do this for me, I will get the both of you a place in the Delegation."

"That seems a little out of your wheelhouse, doesn't it?" Seven asked. "Do you have your father's permission to be offering us something like that?"

I narrowed my eyes.

I wasn't offering *her* anything.

"I don't need my father's permission to offer you anything; just know that my word is bond, and if I'm offering it to then, it's available."

"That isn't enough," Sheldon announced, shaking his head. "And you are well aware of that, so tell me... what else do you have for us?"

"When I decide to make my exit, your daughter will take my place. I'll see to it myself."

Storm Black was only three and already more powerful than any head of any family had ever been. Their daughter would rule every part of the underworld, and no one will be able to stop her. Not me, her parents, or any enemy.

"So, what do you say?" I let my lips curve into a smile and lifted an eyebrow. "Are you with me or not?"

"We would've said yes without the incentives," Monroe said, a smirk on her pretty face. "But now that we have this on the table, we're in."

"Incoming," Jaz called out, alerting us to another visitor.

Even if I wanted to, I couldn't stop the deep sigh from escaping as my body reacted to the idea of seeing Enzo. Almost as if it recognized him as someone important to us.

"Don't worry..." I walked over to the door and unlocked it. "...he's just the other part of my plan."

I quickly got the door open to stop him before he could get to the steps.

"Take that tracker off my car now that you're here," I said, leaning halfway out the door. "Let that be the last time you ever do that."

"I'll think about it," he replied and whistled while retrieving the damn near microscopic device. He lifted it as proof and said, "Am I allowed to enter now?"

I stepped back with the screen door pushed wide open and waved him in.

"Aw, look, we have our own little baby delegation going on here," Seven cooed as I locked the doors and activated the security gate.

"Bianchi," Sheldon greeted, the expression on his face impassive.

"Black," Enzo spoke back. "How's my Goddaughter?"

God Daughter?

"A fucking terrorist," Monroe replied, tossing a cool smile Enzo's way. "And how many times do I have to tell you she isn't your goddaughter?"

He shrugged, and I narrowed my eyes at him and Sheldon, watching in what felt like slow motion as both men smiled. Not a fake lift, and then it's gone, but *real* ones. Then, they embraced like they were fucking friends.

Well, there went my need to make introductions.

"What the fuck is this?"

"I thought you'd figure it out," Enzo said, turning his head to face with a smug smirk planted on it. "You knew everything else about me but didn't think to look into my father and his friends?"

It hadn't because his father wasn't my target, and that was a mistake I'd never make again with this man and his family.

"His father and mine," Monroe clarified. "Chicago has a way of connecting like-minded people."

She gave me a knowing look, and I rolled my eyes.

Chicago had connected us. It had connected my parents as well, but I didn't have time to think about who else this man could be acquainted with that wasn't openly known.

"Let's get to the point," I said, brushing past Enzo.

"Do we not get introductions?" Gaia asked, side-eyeing Enzo as if he were the enemy.

Which, in her defense, he damn well could be.

"No."

I turned back to the map I'd laid out and pointed to where Enzo's casino sat.

"This is how we'll get them out of the tri-state undetected."

Chapter 10

Enzo

"Alright, so you found me," Lucia said, following me outside of their safehouse that sat in the middle of nowhere smackdab on the New Jersey and Pennsylvania border.

"You *let* me find you," I corrected, smirking down at her.

She wasn't dressed in all black today. Instead, she wore a form-fitted long-sleeved red shirt, dark blue jeans, and red Vans on her feet. Lucia stuffed her arms into a leather jacket and then narrowed her eyes.

"I don't know," I went on, pulling open the driver's side door of my truck. "Sounds like you wanted that date after all." I pointed to the passenger side. "Get in."

"I didn't agree to go anywhere today."

"No, you didn't. Take a ride with me anyway. We need to talk."

I ducked into the truck, and by the time I'd started it up and tucked my seatbelt behind my back, she was sliding into the passenger seat, her floral scent filling the space around us and fucking with my mental at the same time.

I took a deep breath and cursed softly under my breath before pulling out of the driveway and onto the road. Being in her presence was fucking with me. It almost made me want to back out of the arrangement I'd gotten both of us into, but the urge to do so would stay just as that. *An urge.*

"Let me guess you ran this by your father, and he wasn't too happy."

"What makes you think I run my moves by my father before deciding on them?"

She scoffed, and I briefly cut my eyes in her direction.

"You may have power, but you don't have the last say."

"Does your father know you're toting guns and planning infiltrations on another family's territory?"

She'd been right.

I hadn't talked to my father, but I could guarantee hers knew nothing of her extracurricular activities. Not when it had to do with their long-lost family.

"My father has no say in how I move outside of his territory."

I could hear the relief in her tone, not the sass she'd been trying to give.

"And why is that?"

"Why is what?"

Instead of clarifying what I meant, knowing that she was well aware, I kept driving until we made it to a private airstrip owned by a family friend. I took the opportunity to steal a glance in Lucia's direction again. She was sitting up straight, her eyes narrowed and scanning the area.

"Nope," she blurted, shaking her head once we came upon my plane—a Hawker 800XP. "Not happening."

It had been my first big purchase. Not a home or a car, but a matte black jet with gold trim and my name etched into the wing—almost undetectable but not to me, and that was all that mattered.

"I'm not going anywhere with you."

"You agreed to take a ride." I parked and opened my door, cutting my gaze over my shoulder at Lucia. "Never took you for someone who'd back down from a little conversation in the air."

Malik appeared at the Jet's entrance and jogged down the stairs.

"We're all cued up to go," he said, never glancing at Lucia but making his interest in who she was known to me by effortless look.

"Malik, this is Lucia Moretti..." I reached out, took her hand, and pulled her closer to my side. "Lucia, this is my—"

"Your guard dog," she mused, smiling up at Malik, who towered over her frame. "That was uncalled for, I apologize," she said right after revealing a little bit of home training.

Malik didn't react, but I'd known he wouldn't. The man wasn't fazed by much of anything but was as deadly as they come. He'd been with me since early adulthood. We were only two years apart—him being the oldest—and I trusted the man with my life and now hers.

"We're going to have to work on that attitude of yours."

"Don't worry about my attitude, Bianchi," she quipped, elbowing me in my ribs so I'd let her hand go.

Laughing, I gripped my side and massaged the area she'd targeted. Malik lifted an eyebrow, and I shook my head. There was nothing to explain at the moment, only that I'd lost my mind over this spitfire of a woman. I watched Lucia saunter up the stairs and onto the jet.

"Don't ask," I warned, handing him my keys. "Keep it right here."

"Enzo—"

"I'm good."

I waved him off before he could convince me to let him on the plane with us. But I needed some time alone with her. To figure out what her motive really was. It was bigger than wanting to save people. In fact, it felt like she was really trying to save herself through others.

"And armed," I added, tapping my waist without looking in his direction. "Sit tight."

I ascended the stairs and was met by a flight attendant with a slight frown on her face.

"Problem?" I asked, angling my head at her.

Her pale skin flushed as she kept cutting her gaze toward the pilot's pit. I didn't need to ask the question again because Lucia appeared from the same direction, a deep frown on her face.

"Why do we need to fly to DC?"

I dismissed the flight attendant, who all but ran off.

"Do you always scare the people you encounter?"

She laughed and walked away, sliding into one of the first seats near the front. I slid into the one directly across from her and pulled my seatbelt on.

"I only asked her a question," she said, picking at her nails. "Had you told me this was what you meant by taking a ride, I wouldn't have had to do that."

She shrugged and continued to pick at her nails, and I sat there staring at her like a fucking creep. She knew it too and ignored my existence until it was announced that we'd be in the air soon, and the plane began to taxi.

When she finally lifted her expressionless eyes to meet mine, we didn't speak. Instead, we held one another's gazes, and the intensity peaked with each second that passed, stirring something inside of me.

"You're going to be a problem," I stated, breaking the silence between us.

"I'm a problem for a lot of people."

"I don't give a fuck about other people. I'm talking about you and me right now. You're going to be a problem for *me*."

She leaned forward and rested her elbows on her knees, a small smile forming on her lips.

"Yet, here I am."

"Here you are."

Lucia rested against her seat again and asked, "Why am I here, Enzo?"

"Did you forget what we agreed to?"

"How could I forget about you helping me with a good cause?"

I smirked.

"You think marrying me is a good cause?" I asked, enjoying the way her body seemed to react to the word. "I'm flattered."

"Haha, the made man knows his way around a joke or two."

I released myself from the confines of my seatbelt, now that we were safely in the air, and grabbed her ankle, which she allowed me to do without an aggressive reaction to it.

"What do you have against made men?"

I brushed my fingers over the simple gold anklet she wore. It wasn't anything significant about it, but she jerked her leg away seconds later as if it were.

"My list is too long for this short ride."

Mmm.

There were many reasons to hate a man of my caliber, but Lucia was bred from a man well above mine. Had a brother she'd shared a womb with who would one day sit where her father was. The disdain for the exact people she'd spent her life with meant it was personal. Not against them or me but everyone else who hadn't seen us as one of them.

We shared the same anger.

"I understand."

The haze in her eyes cleared, showing a brief moment of surprise before it was gone.

"What's the story?"

"Not something I care to discuss at the moment."

"Then..." she paused when I raised up a little, only to settle in my seat again. "What is it that you want to talk about?"

I took my time giving her a response; watching her watch me was more fun.

She couldn't figure me out, anyone more than I could her. Maybe it was the challenge of winning her over, but I knew better. It was her. Not the action to get what I wanted from her but simply *her*.

"Have you ever been in love?" I asked.

She sat unmoving, body stiff as a board.

"No."

Her reply had been quick, a little *too* quick for my liking.

"No?" I slanted my head as if it would help me understand what she really meant. "Neither have I," I confessed, giving her a small piece of me. "Never thought about it until recently."

"Not because of me, I hope."

"Why not because of you?"

She scoffed and quickly removed her seatbelt, standing abruptly right after. Her frustration was clear, and I had no fucking idea why, but I wanted to know every detail.

Fuck.

I think I wanted to save her.

But even that didn't feel right for the way she was presenting herself to me. Lucia wasn't a damsel in distress. She was a fucking siren—a siren I wanted to paint the town red for.

"Look, Enzo," she said, staring down at me like something didn't make sense to her—like *I* didn't make sense. "I'm not here for love or for whatever it is you suddenly want to give me.

This..." she waved between the two of us. "...is a means to an end. Nothing more or less."

"Who are you trying to convince? Me or you?" I asked.

I searched her eyes for something to go on but got nothing, so I rested my head against the seat and closed my eyes.

For a long moment, silence filled the space around us. I could feel her staring a hole into my face but refused to acknowledge her presence. She grumbled something under her breath, and the sound of her dropping into her seat came next. I heard the click of her seatbelt and smirked. We could play the *means to an end* game if she wanted. I was undefeated, but she didn't need to know that, not yet, at least.

We were in the air for less than an hour when the plane began to descend into D.C., and I finally gave her my attention again. She was staring off at nothing in particular, her hair pulled from the bun she'd been wearing and framing her face. I felt her impatience but mostly her curiosity about why I brought her here.

I stood and held my hand out for hers after we were cleared to do so.

She eyed it reluctantly, a smidgen of vulnerability showing on her face.

"Give me a few hours of your time, Lucia. That's all I'm asking for. After this, we can go back to our regularly scheduled programming."

Her gaze met mine, that vulnerability still there, while she searched for anything other than the truth. Eventually, Lucia gave me exactly what I wanted by placing her hand softly into mine.

"Why are we here?"

"I'm taking you on a date like promised."

I waved to the blacked-out SUV and driver waiting for us.

"I'm not dressed for—"

"Don't worry about that," I reassured her, opening the back door after stopping the driver from doing so and helping her inside.

She immediately reached for her seatbelt, and I stopped her, taking it from her hand to secure her in place myself. I leaned over her body more than I needed to.

"I don't want to have to kill you," she whispered, laying her palm against the side of my face. "Don't make me do that."

I found solace in that threat.

"You'll just have to trust me, *Bellissima*," I murmured against the shell of her ear.

"That's not how my world works..." she tugged on my beard, her gaze trained on it while she rolled the hair follicles between her fingers. "I don't have to trust you, but *you* do have to earn it."

I drew back, and she stared ahead, pulling the same stunt I'd pulled on her and ignoring my presence.

"Heard you," I mumbled, shutting her inside.

Heard you loud and clear.

Chapter 11
Lucia

He'd thought of everything. And it burned me up inside to admit that I appreciated his tenacity.

I paced inside of my suite at the White-Hill Hotel Enzo had me in, right in front of the door that led to the room he currently occupied. Was he trying to tempt me? Did he know I hadn't been touched by a man properly in over six months? Why the fuck was I even considering the idea of...

I shook my head and walked over to my phone, picking it up and dialing Gaia.

"What the fuck, Luci," was the first thing out of her mouth after picking up. "Enzo Bianchi had not been discussed."

He hadn't been, but the man had something we could utilize, and I would do anything to have access to it, including marrying him.

"We can talk about that later. I need my cousin for a few moments."

She sighed, and I knew I would have to make it up to her and the girls. Having Monroe and Sheldon involved was completely different than Enzo. They weren't physically going to be in on anything we did. On the other hand, Enzo was more involved now than I'd meant for him to be.

"What's wrong? I saw you leave with him."

"I agreed to a date, and now we're in D.C."

Silence and then laughter filled the line.

"Lucia, I love you, I really do..." she paused to laugh again. "...but sometimes you work my last nerve. What kind of pep talk do you need? One that'll help you be okay bouncing on that man's dick later. Or do we have to have the *other* talk? You know the one I'm referring to."

I knew, and I almost hated her for even thinking to bring it up. Subtle or not. The topic was off-limits to everyone who knew, meaning her.

"I don't need a pep talk."

She snorted, and I hung up, realizing it had been a mistake to call.

Gaia didn't truly understand; no one did.

I was better off keeping my inner thoughts and feelings to myself.

Shortly after, my phone chimed with a text, and I glanced at the screen.

G: *I'm sorry, Luci. That wasn't fair. I have no clue what's going on with you when it comes to Enzo, but if you're already there, just go with it for the night. You can go back to being badass Scarlet later. I love you and be safe. I can't stop Luca from destroying everything in his path if something were to happen to you.*

Noise from the other side of the joining door caught my attention. It was soft but not too low that I couldn't hear the knock.

I quickly typed back, "*I love you, too,*" to Gaia and set my phone on the coffee table. Before acknowledging him, I glanced down at the dress he'd had delivered ten minutes after we arrived.

It was red and short. Silk. With thin straps and a scoop neck that showed off just enough cleavage but not too much. The dress was perfect, right up my alley.

The shoes were still in the box. I hadn't even opened it to see what they looked like. I ignored the designer packaging, begging me to open it, and padded softly across the room to allow him inside after he knocked again.

"I knew red would be your color," he said, regarding me from head to toe. "You look stunning, Lucia."

I raked my gaze over him, refusing to openly show how his compliment made my insides turn to mush. However, I couldn't keep my reaction to his bespoke suit under lock and key. It fit his stature impeccably. He'd even gone with a navy blue shade and white shirt instead of the standard black on black—a small detail I appreciated more than anything.

"You clean up well," I offered, stepping back so he could enter.

He hummed in response, swaggering over to the tan gift bag and matching box next to it with white script lettering across each showcasing the designer's name. I watched him pull the red-soled, black opened-toed strappy heel out and inspect it. Then, he turned and beckoned for me to sit after clearing the chair.

I obliged, and he stood over me for what felt like ages before kneeling and placing one shoe beside us while keeping the other and lifting my right foot. I stared down at him in disbelief.

"Relax," he ordered, slipping the heel on and buckling it around my ankle.

"How'd you know my right size?"

Not only was the dress size correct, but the shoes were too.

"I've been told I have a good eye for small details."

What was this man trying to prove?

I placed my now shoe-clad foot on the floor, and he repeated the same step with my left, securing the shoe and buckle. When Enzo finished, he stayed in his lowered position and observed me.

"Your eyes hold a lot of secrets."

My heart staggered at the softness in his voice. But also at the truth in his statement.

"Will they affect me in any way?"

"Not that I know of," I admitted, feeling inclined to do so.

"If it ever does, will you tell me?"

"It depends."

He hummed and brushed his fingers over my exposed thighs, sending a smattering of chills up and down my arms and across my chest.

Why did that feel so damn good?

"You're trouble, Lucia Moretti," he whispered, repeating those words again. "I'm not sure what kind, but I am sure it'll all come to the light soon enough."

I wanted to move, but my body wouldn't allow it. That raspy baritone kept me rooted in my seat and at his will. If he had spread my legs just then, I would have let him feast on me until he was full.

"Until then," he continued, gaze filled with undeniable lust. "Your secrets belong to you."

"And your secrets?" I found myself asking.

"Can be yours, too. All you have to do is ask."

Enzo stood to his full height, and I took a small breath, welcoming the rush of air into my lungs. I hated the way he made me feel—the way his presence left me unable to breathe.

This wasn't supposed to be happening. Our agreement wasn't supposed to become a breeding ground for anything else. How was I supposed to do this when he made me feel like the possibilities were endless?

"Shall we go?"

He helped me stand and kept my hand in his, pushing his fingers through mine.

It was too intimate, but I couldn't force myself to pull away.

"Where are we going to dinner?"

I'd been to D.C on numerous occasions but never for leisure, always business.

"You'll see," was his response, and the vagueness annoyed me.

I hated surprises. They meant I couldn't be prepared for unknown possibilities.

The same driver from the private airstrip was waiting outside of the hotel for us. We both slipped into the backseat, and the second we were moving, Enzo sat a black suede jewelry box in my lap. I stared at the foreign object, slightly annoyed but intrigued. Maybe a little nervous that it was a ring, and I wasn't ready for that.

"It's not a ring," he said, picking up on my wariness. "Consider it a thank you for trusting me just enough to get on that plane."

I picked up the box and flipped it open.

My heart reacted before I did. Beating uncontrollably at the ruby charm sitting pretty in its confines. It would go perfectly with... I shook my head and shut it.

"I hope you know that you can't buy me, Enzo," I said, not much fire in my tone as I'd wanted.

It was a fine piece of jewelry. Small and significant. It was my style.

I might not have been the typical daughter of a mafia don, but I liked nice things. My father's money never meant much to me, but I had my own, and a lot of it. And though I spent it carefully, I still bought myself luxury items from time to time.

"While crazy, I agreed to marry you..." I cut my eyes at him, finding his already burning into me. "I need to be treated as an equal, not some princess you hide away in a tower and drip in jewels for your enemies to see on occasion."

His lips twitched, and then he let it out, chuckling deep from his gut. The sound filled me up and warmed my body from head to toe. He had a nice laugh. One that would be memorable. If I heard it in a crowded room, I would know it was him immediately.

"Am I a joke to you?"

"No, Lucia..." he shook his head, the amusement gone and replaced with something dark. "But I do find it funny that you'd think I could look at you and assume buying you the finest things in life would impress you. Or even place me on your good side, for that matter. When the truth is much simpler than that."

"Enlighten me on the truth..."

He picked up the box and opened it, removing the jewel and holding it up for us both to see.

"I saw something that reminded me of you and couldn't leave without it. It has a sharp cut like your eyes. A standout is what it is, what *you* are."

He looked into my eyes, and I shifted in my seat, trying my best to ease the ache forming between my thighs. That passion in his voice... it did something to my insides.

"Why'd you pick a charm?" I asked, taking it from him after deciding that I would accept it. "I don't have anything to put it on."

"You have somewhere," he said as our car came to a stop outside of True Steakhouse.

I'd never been but heard nothing but great things. It was a

spot known to be frequented by many state representatives or government officials. I knew for my own reasons but Enzo bringing me here almost felt like a setup for something else. Not just a date but business too.

That made me feel a way, but I wouldn't admit it to him or anyone for that matter. Instead, I put the ruby back into his safe haven and slipped it into my clutch purse.

Enzo got out and walked around to open my door. When he stopped me and kneeled, I had my foot out of the car.

"Hand it here," he requested, tone brokering no argument.

So, I did just that and watched as he attached it to my anklet that indeed was meant for charms. I'd snatched them all off a while ago, tossing the expensive pieces into the trash after learning how they'd been acquired.

"See..." he stood tall and helped me out completely. "Feels like it was meant to be."

He had no idea what he'd just done to me. To my stupid heart.

I had no intention of allowing this man to dazzle or worm his way into the off-limit parts of me.

We were quickly ushered to our seat upon entering, a spot toward the back of the restaurant that gave us a view of every corner and table. The lighting was bright enough to admire the chic décor but still low enough for two people to enjoy an intimate dinner together.

"Mr. Bianchi, your server will be over right away," the hostess informed us before heading back to her station.

"You've been here before?"

"Once or twice..."

"Mmm, I see."

He stared at me from across the table like he'd miss something I might say if he looked away. Like he was drawn to me as I was to him. I should've been wary of him, as I was with most men, but I couldn't help but feel intrigued, more like a magnet in search of something to stick to, preferably the man across from me.

A sommelier approached our table. I could tell the difference by her attire. The servers were dressed in black—pants, and shirts, while this woman was also in black; she was in a dress with heels that were about five inches on her feet.

"Red or white?" Enzo asked, his gaze locked with mine.

I took my eyes from his, needing a moment to breathe, and placed them on the sommelier. She had kind eyes, but I'd learned years ago that the kindest people had seen the worst of the worst yet still found a way to be good to others.

"I'm partial to red, but I think I'm open to trying something new."

She smiled and nodded.

"How about we sample a few?"

I glanced at Enzo for approval and almost cursed at the way I'd done it without thinking. I didn't need his approval, yet here I was seeking it.

"I'm following your lead," he mused, resting against the booth with a lazy grin on his face.

"Let's have a few samples."

Our sommelier disappeared and came back with two trays holding three small stemless wine glasses—all filled with a small tasting amount of wine. Two red and one white. She placed one in front of me and the other in front of Enzo.

"On the far left is our house Pinot Noir and my personal favorite. It's versatile, pairing well with pork and red meat."

I picked up the glass at the same time as Enzo, twirling it around before sniffing and then bringing it to my lips. I'd never been good at figuring out the notes, but I liked to pretend I knew what I was doing.

"The acidity is perfect for that expensive steak you plan to order," Enzo said, setting his glass down and reaching for the one in the middle. "It has a nice fruity taste but is not too overbearing that you'll miss its earthiness."

To say he'd shocked me was an understatement.

My pussy thumped, and I squeezed my thighs together, praying he couldn't sense my arousal.

"Shall we try the rest?"

I shook my head and glanced at our sommelier, who wore a knowing smile on her face.

"Pinot Noir it is," she said, taking our floats.

"The bottle," Enzo added before she got too far away.

"What do you want from me?" I blurted, the words falling from my lips before I could stop them.

"I *didn't* want anything until you invaded my space and came asking for something from *me*."

Touché.

"And now?" I pressed.

"Well, now I want everything you're willing to offer."

"What about the things I'm not willing to give?"

"That's a bridge we'll cross when we get there, Lucia."

I sneered at that, and his lips curved.

"Not if I burn it down first."

Enzo leaned into the table, his gaze smoldering. For a brief moment, he didn't speak, waiting patiently for our wine to be placed on the table by the server that appeared.

"Burning it down won't deter me. I have the means to rebuild."

He relaxed in his seat again, like he hadn't said anything of significance. Then he turned to the server, who seemed to understand that now wasn't the time to speak, and said, "She'll have the most expensive steak on the menu. A tomahawk, I believe. Asparagus and the red skin potato mash..." he eyed me for approval, and I nodded. "I'll have what she's having."

There went that thumping in my chest again.

What it sounded like he meant was, *I'll have her.*

Enzo Bianchi was nothing like I'd expected or researched; I knew I was in trouble. And it wouldn't be anyone else's fault but my own.

"Tell me why we're really *here.*"

He smirked and looked at something over my shoulder that made me want to turn but instead, I kept my gaze on him.

"He just walked in."

Chapter 12

Enzo

Eventually, her curiosity got the best of her, and she turned to see who'd I been speaking of, only to find that he and the rest of his party weren't visible any longer.

"What kind of game are you playing?"

I checked my watch for the time.

"The long one," I said, standing. "Shall we go introduce ourselves before our food arrives?"

I took her hand without asking this time, giving her no choice but to stand and follow me to the private dining room on the other side of the restaurant. The doors were drawn shut, and the guard standing on the outside stood a little taller the closer I got.

"Tell Senator Michaels I'd like to see him, and he has about two seconds to make that happen. I'd love to embarrass him in front of all these people."

I waved my free hand around for emphasis.

"One."

He moved to the side, already knowing who I was and what

I was capable of. I lifted an eyebrow, and he slid the doors open, revealing three men. All three holding a position of power that people like me exploited but none of them were innocent.

"Gentlemen," I greeted, sliding the door shut and releasing Lucia so she could take in what was happening under her father's nose.

"What is this?" Novice Buck spat out, his face turning an ugly shade of red.

His hatred for me was comical. It was too bad Pietro sent his stand-in and hadn't brought himself to the party. Novice was nothing but a pawn in a bigger scheme.

"I heard congratulations are in order." I pulled up a seat and reached out to slide the plate of scallops my way. "Who knew the head of the Pennsylvania labor union was tied to the mafia?"

Henry Malfoy, who had been stopping all permit requests submitted by the Moretti team for their new housing project, looked perturbed and a little afraid. I wasn't buying the innocent act. He knew exactly who Leonardo Moretti was, just as he knew who Novice was tied to. Anyone who was smart would have played their cards right and chosen the better team to be on, but here he was sitting with a state representative who had a bad rap and the liaison to the sick fuck who brought Lucia to my doorstep in the first place.

I'd have to thank him for that one day.

When Lucia said her father had an issue that mine could take care of as a way into the Delegation, I did some digging, and it turned out Leonardo's own *father* was working against him. And I use that term lightly. Pietro was more of a sperm donor in this instance. A deadbeat.

I popped a scallop into my mouth and chewed, enjoying the burst of flavor.

"Did you know that scallops come in a shell? Like clams? It's quite interesting—"

"What do you want?" Senator Michaels asked, flexing his jaw in anger.

"Do you see that pretty woman over there?" I pointed to Lucia, whose gaze was curiously pinned on me. "Well, she's going to be my wife one day soon, and I figured I'd give her the perfect engagement gift today."

I stood up and circled back to where she stood.

"Here's how this is going to go," I said, pulling out a white envelope from inside my suit jacket and tossing it onto the table. "Henry here is going to take these photos and pick a new team to do bad things for. Or maybe it's best you do your job the correct way seeing as the Moretti's submitted their documents in that manner without trying to bribe you. We'd appreciate that more than anything. Take your pick."

"You can't—"

"Senator Michaels don't forget where you reside or the things I know about you. I can guarantee the Costas won't be able to save you from the hell I'll bring down on your office."

I never took my eyes off Lucia.

She was fucking beautiful—so much so that I'd rather she be around from now on when I'm conducting business. She was dressed to the nines with that gun tucked in the holster high up on her thigh.

"I need those Moretti permits approved by mid-day tomorrow, or none of you will like what comes next."

"This is a death sentence," Novice spat as if his threat would faze me.

He couldn't touch me even if he begged Pietro Costa himself. There were rules, channels to go through, and even then, he'd have a hard time making it happen. But I was itching for him to try.

"We're all living on borrowed time, gentleman. Use yours wisely. I know I am."

"You're marrying a Costa," Novice went on, trying his hand at taunting Lucia. "Doesn't matter what last name your father took on," he spewed, aiming his frustration in her direction. "We share the same blood. It'd be best *you* remember that."

I pulled my gun and pointed it at his head. The room was silent; I could hear their hearts beating in anticipation of what I would do next. I closed the distance between Lucia and me, leaned down, and whispered into her ear, "I'll kill him now; all you have to do is say the word."

Where Novice fucked up was forgetting that I wasn't under the Commission's reign anymore. And even if I were, killing him would be worth the consequences.

Lucia stared up at me as if I'd somehow cracked the code to what she really needed. Her eyes were filled with appreciation and something else much darker. Something right up my alley.

"Maybe another day," she said, her lips lifting slowly at the corners. "I'm hungry."

"You fellas have a nice dinner..." I tucked my gun and took her hand, reaching around her to slide the door open. "On me," I added. "I'm in a good mood tonight."

I was in a really good fucking mood.

After dinner, Lucia and I strolled the strip the restaurant sat on. My driver, who really dubbed as the security Malik set up while Lucia and I were in the air, drove slowly beside us.

"Why not ask your brother for help?"

"My brother has other responsibilities."

I cut my eyes at her.

"And I don't?"

"You have an underground tunnel, my brother has a lot of things, but a tunnel isn't one of them."

She had a point, and I wasn't one to deny the truth when it was right in front of me.

"Touché."

We came to the end of the block, and I stopped, glancing around before taking her hands into mine. She regarded me; the shutters lifted from her eyes just a little.

"Getting married doesn't need to happen," I said, saying what I'd been thinking all night aloud. "My resources are yours."

"Out of the kindness of your heart, huh?"

She didn't look convinced, and I wouldn't try getting her there. Forcing her to marry me because my dick got a little hard at the darkness inside of her made me no better than the men she wanted to stop.

"Nah." I shook my head and released her hand, waving for the driver to pull in front of us. "Just proving that there's some good inside of me somewhere."

"That's too bad," she cooed, walking over to the door without waiting for my assistance. "Because we already agreed, and backing out isn't an option. I'll send word to my father about what you did."

She opened the door and slid inside, moving over to make room for me.

"Come on, future husband, we have shit to do. People to see. Businesses to destroy."

I chuckled and got in.

Fuck it.

I was game to do a little destroying, especially with this woman who seemed to have more secrets than every department in the united states government combined.

"There's one more thing I'd like to address."

"Oh yeah?" I hit the button to close the divider and block the driver from seeing and hearing us.

"And what would that be?"

"You'll want heirs, right?"

I cut my eyes at her and nodded.

In this world, having an heir to take your place was expected of you once married. My father had never beat the idea of it into my head growing up because he moved differently, but I wanted one of my own—a family.

"What are you getting at?"

She turned her body, placing her back against the door, her legs onto the space between them, and spread wide for me. Beneath that little red dress, she donned a gun strapped to her left leg and a pair of flesh-colored lace panties. They were drenched in her arousal, and it took everything in me not to reach over and cop a feel.

"Maybe we should test out this chemistry between us."

I licked my lips, my gaze still hyper-focused on the outline of her fat pussy lips being on display for me. I looked into her eyes briefly, and what I'd been looking for was already staring back at me.

"Come here," I commanded, tugging her by the arm until she was positioned in my lap.

I pulled her body against mine and secured her by the waist. She hummed softly after feeling I, too, was turned on by her. Not by the fact that she'd offered herself but by *her* in general. Lucia fucked with my head, but I wasn't against this type of mind game.

"Tell me something, Ms. Moretti." I gripped the back of her neck, gently pressing my thumb into her pulse point. Her heart rate was up but somehow still steady. Like she was prepared for however this would go. I liked that shit. "How do you like to be fucked?"

Her lips parted, but no words escaped, and she looked

away. With my left hand still on her neck, I tipped her head back with the other forcing her gaze to meet mine again.

"Say it."

"I'm not sure if what I used to like will be sufficient enough with you," she admitted, her voice low and heated and dripping with pure sex. "I don't think we have enough time to figure that out."

"We have enough time for whatever the fuck I say we have enough for."

Her eyes darkened, and I went for it, greedily stealing the kiss I'd been thinking about since she showed up at the casino. Lucia melted into me and whispered into my mouth, "Just a small little taste."

At first, I kissed her slowly, teasing, but it quickly turned into fervor. Lucia trembled against me, her hands pressed against my chest before she slid them up and around my neck. I tightened my hold around her waist in response, brushing my fingers up the curve of her ass. She moaned, her lips parting, and I slid right in, tangling and stroking my tongue against hers, igniting the fire building in the both of us.

The intensity was raw, primal.

Her moans vibrated through me.

Her scent was intoxicating and mixed in with the small buzz from the wine we'd drunk—an entire bottle almost. Lucia rolled her pussy against my erection, dragging it back and forth. She quickened the motion, and her moans grew louder in my mouth.

I slipped my hands into her dress, pulling it up over her waist and allowing the silky fabric to rest against my arms.

"You're intoxicating."

"Let me get you drunk then," she whispered back, her chest heaving.

I smiled, knowing what I was about to do was going to piss her off but also be a slight punishment for myself.

"We're out of time, baby," I told her, pulling back just enough that our lips weren't touching anymore. "It's time to go home."

I gestured toward the private jet, clueing her in that we'd made it to our destination. The plan had never been to stay in D.C.

Everything we'd left at the hotel was gathered by the driver while we were at dinner.

Her eyes still filled with heat, she smirked.

"Who says we don't have time?" she questioned, placing her lips up against my ear. "You could always introduce me to the mile-high club."

Then, she opened the door and climbed out, right from my lap, adjusting her dress and sauntering toward the plane without a backward glance. I wasted no time following behind her after addressing the driver and thanking him for his service.

Lucia was seated in the same place she'd been on the way here. I took her hand and kept walking, knowing she would have no choice but to stand and come with me. The first door we came upon, I dragged her into it.

She turned and stared at me through the bathroom mirror, slightly bent over and inviting me to do as I pleased with her.

I took a few deliberate steps, pressing my erection into the curve of her ass and grasping her hips. After I aligned my body with hers, Lucia let out a soft gasp and I pressed my lips just below her ear, brushing them against her soft flesh. I took a deep breath, purposely drowning myself in her scent again. She smelled so goddamn good, enough to drive a sane man out of his fucking mind.

"Has it been a long time?"

I asked, but the truth was I didn't give a fuck.

"Long enough."

I squeezed her hips and slid my hands down, gathering the hem of her dress and pulling it up. I inserted my foot between hers, and she widened her stance without protest.

"Good girl," I murmured into her neck, brushing my fingers up and down her bare thigh.

She moaned, and I smirked, staring at her in the mirror.

Lucia stared back at me, daring me to go further with the raise of her brow. And so I did, dragging my thumb over the seat of her lace panties before pulling them to the side. I kissed softly down from her ear, along her jaw, and the side of her neck. Her breathing grew more erratic, and she leaned back against me, trusting me to hold her as she slowly unraveled.

I wrapped my free arm around her mid-section for added security while teasing her clit without touching it just yet. She was wet and trembling with need. I was hard as a fucking brick but fucking her in this bathroom wouldn't be how our first encounter went. So, I settled for something else.

"You want me to take that edge off for you?" I whispered huskily. Slowly, I circled her nub. "Give you a nice little orgasm before we take off?"

"Why can't I have more?" Her voice shook as she spoke.

I chuckled and sped up my movements.

"You don't think I'm going to fuck you in this bathroom for our first time, do you?"

Her pussy went from damp to soaked, and I groaned, my dick straining in my pants.

Fuck.

"You like that idea? Me treating this pussy the way it deserves to be?"

Another small moan escaped her, and her hips hitched forward, pressing into the stroke and slide of my finger, greedy for more.

"I want verbal answers, Princess." My voice was a low, demanding growl.

"Y-yes," Lucia whispered, her head falling back on my shoulder. "I-I like that idea."

"I thought you might. You're a woman who shouldn't settle for anything less." I kept playing with making her grind brazenly against just the one finger I was giving her access to. "And I'm more than happy to give that to you."

There was a part of me that wanted to move forward in this, to plunge my fingers into her pussy and get her nice and open and ready to be fucked, but I wasn't going to win her over with a quickie, nor was I built for them. I preferred taking my time when I was interested enough to do so, and Lucia had all of my attention.

I scraped my teeth against the line of her jaw, and Lucia squirmed, trapped between my body and the counter. My finger grazed back and forth, trying to find that one spot—and I knew when I found it, Lucia's whole body seized up a little, her hips jerking forward.

"Mmm," I crooned, flicking my thumb right up against her clit. "You really need this, don't you?"

Lucia panted while trying to shove her hips down onto the pad of my thumb, seeking more pressure and friction. Her nails scraped against the countertop. "E-Enzo...."

I massaged a little harder, removing my thumb and adding two fingers this time, rubbing in concentrated circles. I'd always found it a fun challenge to see how I could get a woman off with specific methods instead of just plowing my dick into her like some teenage boy who'd never had pussy before. And the idea that Lucia was so keyed up that it would take only this to get her off was possibly the sexiest shit I'd ever experienced. Lucia moaned, louder this time, and I relished the victory. I nipped at her pulse point, and she shivered.

"Oh, you like that?" I whispered. "You like a little teeth?"

"Yes," she admitted, her voice breathy.

This time, I bit down a little harder, still strumming her with my fingers, and brought my other hand up to pinch her nipple through her dress. Lucia gasped, her whole body going stiff, and then she cried out as a rush of slick moisture drenched my finger as she came long and hard, those pussy juices coating the inside of her thighs.

I looked at my watch and then into her sated expression in the mirror, feeling smug suddenly. I fixed her panties, pulled her dress down, and then wrapped both of my arms around her. I held her against my chest until her breathing evened out and she could stand on her own.

"Time for takeoff, baby."

Chapter 13
Lucia

Present

"There you are," Gaia all but yelled, rushing toward Enzo and me as we returned to the backyard.

Her shoes were off, and if she were a shade or two lighter, her skin would be flush red. I could see the frustration and annoyance dancing all over her pretty face. Or maybe she'd been enjoying the open bar a little too much.

"Glad to see you two aren't doing that weird '*we don't know one another*' thing anymore," she added, pointing to our joined fingers. "But, I need to borrow her."

She took my hand from his and pulled me away.

I glanced at Enzo over my shoulder but turned away before being able to decipher the expression he wore.

"What's the problem?"

"Dance with me." She stepped directly in front of me and took my other hand. "I'm just checking on you. Making sure you're okay."

My chest warmed at that.

"I'm okay. This is nothing like I expected but I'm in it."

She shook her head, eyes wide.

"I can't believe you agreed to marry that man. Though, I do hope his dick game makes this whole thing worthwhile. You deserve good dick."

We stared at one another and then burst into laughter.

"I could go," she offered, smoothly changing subjects. "You know I can handle myself."

"We aren't working today. No surveillance."

I didn't doubt her ability, but it was my job to protect her, Jaz, and Violet. They were doing this for me, *with* me. And if we moved, we did it together. That would never be up for debate.

She sighed.

"Leave it be for now. Have another drink."

"We—"

"G..." I wrapped my arms around her until we were chest to chest. "I know you're passionate about this," I whispered against her ear. "And I understand why, I do. But we have to be smart. I can't do this without you. I need you alive and well." I pulled back to see her face. "Alright?"

She nodded, and I shook my head.

"I need to hear you say it."

Gaia rolled her eyes, a smile pulling at her lips. I knew she wasn't happy about my decision, but she also knew that I was right.

"Okay, I won't do anything stupid."

I pulled back and smiled at her.

"You're in a good mood," she pointed out, swinging us around as the song changed.

I was glad I'd decided to skip out on wearing heels and opted for a pair of flats shoes. They couldn't be seen under the weight and size of my dress either way.

"I don't know how I feel," I admitted, looking around at the people watching Gaia and I dance. "This isn't me."

She frowned.

"What isn't you? Being happy about something other than..." she didn't finish her statement, but she hadn't needed to. "Your whole life, you've been trying to keep up with the boys, not even realizing you've surpassed them. It's alright to want to conquer something else, Luci."

She turned me before I could respond and said, "Look at that."

Enzo was dancing with my mother, and from what I could tell, they were having a deep conversation. One that seemed to end with a smile from both of them. She wasn't easy to please. In fact, she'd always said the man who got to have me this way would have to deal with her. And even though this wasn't supposed to be more than a business transaction, she still found a way to get her say.

"All I'm saying is that this life is hectic enough," Gaia said, reminding me that she was still with me. "Why not find love in the midst of it all."

I detected a hint of sadness in her tone and turned to figure out where it came from, but she was already walking away. A light breeze passed, and I could feel eyes on me at that moment. My skin prickled with awareness, and then his breath was a whisper against my neck.

"You're the center of attention, *Bellissima*."

"Maybe they're looking at you," I quipped, turning to face him.

He regarded me closely.

"Only to get to you," he surmised, placing his hands low on my hips and pulling me close.

I lifted my hands and rested them gently against his shoulders. The DJ announced our first dance, and even more, eyes turned in our direction. Being the center of attention had never been my thing. It was bothersome, to say the least.

"Impossible..." I shook my head, hating how true the next words out of my mouth felt to me. "I'm merely the daughter of a mafioso, the twin to his heir, and the wife to another."

"Is that how you see yourself?"

"I see myself as a lot of things, but the first two are a big part of me. It's how most of the people here see me."

I realized how much we still didn't know about each other. It had felt as if we'd known one another for longer than nine months. And a lot of that time we'd spent apart, handling our responsibilities. When we were together, though? Magnetic.

Glasses clinking loudly filled the air, distracting Enzo from responding to me—something I appreciated. They kept going, a few chanting for us to kiss. Enzo's lips twitched as he dipped forward, bringing his mouth mere inches from mine.

"Shall we give the people what they want?"

Instead of responding, I closed the small distance and pressed my lips against his. Quick and chaste. Enough to satisfy our guests but tease the fuck out of us.

Cheers erupted.

The liquor had clearly been flowing, and the party around us was now in full swing. As the sunset was on the horizon, Enzo brought me closer, drowning out the people who had joined us.

"For what it's worth," he whispered against the shell of my ear as we rocked back and forth. "The moment I laid eyes on you, I saw a woman who'd set herself apart from being *just* a mafioso's daughter and the twin to his heir. I saw a woman with power and a brazen enough personality to find herself tangled up with the likes of me. You are not *just* anything, Lucia Bianchi; you are *everything*. And I can guarantee that even though they aren't saying it, every mothafucka in this room can feel it. It's why they can't keep their eyes off you, same as me."

I felt them.

The lingering gazes were hidden behind the guise of good drinks and company. The scrutiny of me—of Enzo and what our union could possibly mean for them. I could taste the disdain of every man who wouldn't benefit from us. And as bitter as it was on my tongue, the exhilarating feeling that followed made it all worth it.

"Hey, Enzo," I murmured, pulling away but only enough to see his face.

"Yeah?"

"I'm ready to stop pretending now."

He took a deep breath, like he wanted to savor those words for a moment, and then said, "How fast do you think we can make it out of here?"

I opened my mouth to respond, but the looming frame standing behind him caught my attention, and I cut my eyes over his shoulder to see who it was.

"Not fast enough," I mumbled. "I think Giovanni is ready to have that talk."

Giovanni Bianchi was going to be a fucking problem for me. He was a pest with an unknown agenda, and that made him dangerous.

"What can we do for you, Gio?" Enzo asked, never turning to face him.

"A dance," he replied, suspiciously calm. "If she'll have me."

Enzo tensed, his fingers gripping my hips a little tighter as he raised a brow in question.

He was giving me a choice, even if his uncle's request hadn't really been one. The man didn't see me as an equal. He might've been the one person in the room who didn't see me the way Enzo figured everyone else did. But I knew how to handle men like him just fine.

"Of course," I spoke softly, releasing Enzo.

He stepped reluctantly to the side, and Giovanni came forward, placing his hands high on my waist. I rested my hands on his shoulders, the same as I had with Enzo, but this felt different. He was a conniving man. I could feel and see it clear as day.

He was the type of man I killed for a living.

"Your father must be proud," he said, staring down at me with those black pools he called eyes.

"Depends on what you think he should be proud of."

He smiled wickedly.

"He went from a small whisper to being the most talked-about boss in a matter of a few months. All because his daughter managed to tie herself to my nephew. He must be proud of all the connections you've brought him."

"Seeing as I had nothing to do with this union, your assumption would be incorrect. But, thank you for having so much faith in me."

He narrowed his eyes at my sarcastic response.

"I see," I went on, holding his gaze with a narrowed one of my own. "You think I'm a fake? That I wiggled my way into your nephew's bed and convinced him to wed me so my father could do, what exactly?"

"If I was your father, I would want revenge."

"Well..." we moved in a slow circle, changing directions. "It's a good thing you aren't my father then, isn't it?"

"Mind your manners, Ms. Moretti," he said through gritted teeth as he dug his fingers into my ribs. "I don't take too kindly to disrespectful women who don't know their place."

The pain shot through me, but I kept my face neutral. I

would never satisfy him by reacting. I stepped into him, my lips curling into a sneer.

"And what place is that?" I asked, pressing my thumb firmly into the dip right beneath his shoulder blade and the curve of his armpit. He tensed up, the pain I was applying flashing in his eyes. "In the shadow of a man?" I pressed harder until he loosened his grip on my ribs. "Giovanni, watch how *you* speak to me. I could kill you with my bare hands if I wanted."

I released him, and he raised his hand to hit me, bringing it down so quickly that I almost missed Enzo coming from our left. His fist connected with Giovanni's jaw, and then his gun was at his head before I had the chance to blink.

"That's how you want to play it, Unc?" Enzo asked, tipping his head to the side in disbelief. "Raising your hand to my wife?"

Everyone was watching, bodies rushing forward and surrounding us.

"Whoa," Angelo spoke, making his presence known. "Son, now isn't the time."

Matteo appeared next, with my father and Luca on their heels. Giovanni's guards had pulled him back, their guns drawn, which only prompted Matteo to do the same. I caught the wave for their guards to stand down.

I was itching to reveal my own gun, but I'd done enough.

"Your *wife* needs to be taught about respect."

"Watch how you speak about my daughter," my father warned. "Remember where you are."

"Is this how you treat guests in your home, Leonardo?"

His eyes were on me, though, a promise of retribution for embarrassing him in them.

I smirked.

"Is this how you treat my home, Giovanni? By disrespecting my daughter? Me?"

I cut my eyes at Enzo.

His gaze was pinned to Giovanni, his jaw set and body stiff. I willed him to look at me, to give me the second I needed to bring him down. He said he would kill for me, and he proved in D.C. that he would do it no matter the consequences but after asking me first.

"Ask me," I said, loud enough to catch his attention and everyone else's too.

Dark shadows danced in his eyes as he brought them to me. This was a part of him I hadn't experienced before. He was here, but he wasn't. Something was keeping him from blacking out completely.

"Ask me," I repeated, taking a step forward only for one of my father's men to step in and reach for me.

"Don't touch her," Enzo growled, his gaze never leaving mine. "All you have to do is say the word."

"Maybe another time. Now doesn't feel right, don't you think?"

I hadn't needed to say more.

He lowered his gun immediately and held his empty hand out to me. I went to him, placing my palm in his. And then, not even a second later, he raised the gun again and shot one of Giovanni's guards in the head.

The pop filled the air, followed by a few squeals from guests.

This was bad.

Very *fucking* bad.

"Don't even try it," Luca boomed, his gun now drawn.

There were multiple pointing at Giovanni and the last guard standing—who wouldn't move without his word. And being that he was outnumbered, I could guarantee he wouldn't push his luck any further than he already had. Not when he was so far outside of his territory.

"I think it's time for you to go," Angelo said, stepping forward. "This won't end well if you don't."

"Is that a threat?"

"A promise," he said, ever so composed.

No bass or hostility in his voice.

He was the epitome of unbothered.

Eventually, Giovanni bowed out, but I knew it wouldn't be the last we heard of him. No one moved until he was gone, Angelo and my father following them out.

"What the fuck was that?" Luca asked, pointing to the dead body.

"I don't answer to you, Moretti," Enzo said after tugging me away in the middle of Luca speaking. "Matteo, handle that. Y'all be easy."

He didn't stop until we were out in the driveway and in front of his truck. Enzo snatched the passenger door open and helped me inside, followed by the rest of my dress. Then he shut me in and strode around to get in. We were off, passing the guards and our fathers out of the already open gate.

"Enzo..."

"Give me a minute."

I could hear the growl in his throat.

That composure he'd had was disappearing and uncovering the monster beneath.

"What did he do?" he questioned after a few moments of silence.

"Dug his fingers into my ribs."

He hit the steering wheel and said something I couldn't quite catch in Italian.

"And?"

"And that's it..." I stared straight ahead. "I mean after I applied pressure to his brachial plexus."

He didn't reply, just drove us in complete silence until we reached my condo. It wouldn't be mine after today. Most of my things had been delivered to Enzo's already and replaced with Jaz and Violet's.

"You make me reckless," he said, pulling into the garage after the magnetic sensor he'd somehow gotten was scanned.

"I'm not reckless."

"What do you want me to do about that, Enzo? Stop being myself?"

He got out and came around to help me, but it felt more like an opportunity for him to mull over how he would reply.

"No, Lucia..." he reached into the truck and grabbed my neck, pulling me halfway out but keeping me upright with his body. "I want you to say the word when I ask. If I'm going to be reckless for you, let me go all the fucking way."

He glared down at me and then smashed his lips into mine. The kiss was bruising, almost feeling like a punishment for not allowing him to kill Giovanni—a made man—in the middle of our reception. An offense that wouldn't go unpunished. He wanted me to let him start a war because I'd been disrespected. My clit throbbed, and I kissed him back, just as hard.

"Enzo," I whimpered into his mouth. "Please take me inside."

He pulled me all the way out of his truck, shut the door, and then led us over to the garage entrance. After getting the door open with a key I *hadn't* given him, he lifted me into his arms bridal style and carried me over the threshold—kicking the door shut behind us.

"Let's see how fast I can get you out of this."

Yes, please!

Chapter 14

Enzo

Somebody had to take the brunt of the anger boiling over inside of me.

And Lucia being the reason I was out of sorts and ready to murder my fucking uncle, made her the perfect victim. It wasn't her fault, but that logical thinking only came when it was time for me to react.

He deserved a bullet to the head. Getting away with disrespecting my wife? That was an open invitation for other made men to do the same and over my dead fucking body.

"What am I going to do with you?" I murmured against Lucia's neck from behind. "Mmm?"

I kissed the length of her bare shoulder while pulling the zipper down on her dress, peeling the material from her skin. She whimpered as I grazed the curve of her back with the tips of my fingers, following the outline of her spine.

"Maybe you need to be taught a lesson," I mused more to myself but garnered a breathless sigh and whimper from Lucia. "Oh. You want that?"

She nodded and attempted to glance at me over her shoulder.

"I need words," I ordered, releasing my hold on her and letting the fabric fall away from her body and pool at her feet. *Damn.*

Everything about this woman was a work of art. The curve of her body, the dips in her waist, and the swell of her hips where the stretch marks I found myself obsessed with sat.

What I'd thought was multiple tattoos covering her abdomen was really just a lone peacock curving up the right side of her body. It was sexy.

I slapped her ass and circled around while releasing the buttons on my dress shirt.

"Words, Luci."

"Yes," she whispered, staring at me in anticipation of what I'd do next.

I continued to work the buttons on my shirt, eyeing the gun strapped to her toned thigh. It was her favorite hiding place and slowly becoming mine—when it was her doing it. She was in a flesh-colored thong that was barely visible against her mahogany skin and no bra, giving me the perfect view of her breasts and nipples raised to stiff peaks.

"Yes, what?"

She pulled her bottom lip between her teeth and narrowed her eyes at me.

Mmm. There she was.

Lucia didn't just *take* anything.

You had to earn her submission, and I loved every fucking minute of doing just that.

"Yes, what?" I repeated, removing my belt and then looping it together again, loose enough to adjust easily.

Her eyes flickered with want, and I smirked.

"What am I saying yes to again?" she asked, flexing her fingers. "I was..." her gaze lifted to meet mine. "...*distracted*."

I raised an eyebrow and beckoned her forward, and she obliged but only by a small margin. Because I knew she'd stand her ground with the small space between us, I closed the distance, her nipples now brushing up against my chest. My spine tingled from the sensation of having her skin just barely touching mine.

I backed her into the bench directly in front of her bed, giving her no choice but to sit. And then, I kneeled in front of her—pushing her legs apart just enough to fit in between.

"Mmm," I hummed, pulling in a deep breath and savoring the smell of her arousal. "You smell fucking divine."

"Enzo..."

I ignored the plea in her tone and pulled the small pistol from her thigh holster, stashing it in the empty space beside her.

"Say it..." I kissed the inside of her thigh and continued up with my eyes on hers. "...and I'll reward her."

Lucia's breathing picked up as I kissed her pussy through her thin panties.

"Yes," she moaned, breathless. "I want to be taught a lesson."

I tapped her right leg, and she knew exactly what to do, lifting it and resting the heel of her foot on my shoulder. I pushed the other to the side, making more room to slide in close. Using my index and middle finger, I stroked her pussy through the soft material. She rolled her hips into it, silently begging for more pressure.

"Oh my..."

Pulling her panties to the side, I flicked her clit with my thumb and then buried my face between her thighs. Then, slowly dragged my tongue up and down her pussy, drowning myself in her essence. She tasted like a grown-ass woman—my *woman*.

"Please, Enzo," she begged, her hooded gaze on me and her arms spread the length of the bed, with her fingers digging into the comforter. "I-I need more."

I knew exactly what she needed, but that didn't mean she'd get it right away.

We were moving on my time, at my speed.

With the tip of my tongue, I slowly teased her clit—focusing solely on it. I flicked the nub, slow and then fast—repeating the motion and making her a whimpering mess. Lucia tried grabbing my head, forcing me to pull away and use the belt I'd prepared just for that.

"You don't get to run this show, baby," I told her, taking her hand and looping the belt around them. "And you know how much I love it when you take charge..." I tightened the leather until it dug into her skin. "Now we both have to suffer."

I tugged her forward by the restraint until we were nose to nose. With my free hand, I stroked her pussy, pushing one finger and then another inside of her. She flexed around my digits, her breathing coming out in short spurts.

"Two months," I murmured against her mouth, straining to keep myself in check. "No call. No text." I worked my fingers in a 'come here' motion, unhurried. "A fucking pigeon carrier would have sufficed."

She kissed me instead of responding, sucking my bottom lip into her mouth. But that wouldn't be enough for me. Lucia hadn't told me she was a Red. That was a little fact I learned for the first time in her father's office and while I'd acted cool about it, what it meant for us burned me up inside.

I drove my fingers into her faster, harder. Taking my anger out on her slick walls.

Her moans grew into sexy whimpers, and I smirked, latching onto the tip of her ear and tugging softly.

"You better not fucking cum either," I growled into her ear.

"E-Enzo..."

I snatched my fingers out of her just as she was on the brink of doing exactly what I'd forbade. Lucia cried out, and I gripped her neck, squeezing it just enough to garner labored breathing. Deep, sexy huffs as she stared at me with disdain.

"Say, please, *Bellissima*."

She squirmed, baring her teeth at me but ultimately giving in to the moment.

"P-Please."

I pushed my fingers into her again and resumed my torture, deliberately tapping her walls.

"I'm sorry," she whispered, looking me in my eyes. "I..." her lids fluttered shut and then opened again after I sped up my movements. "I had to."

I knew why now, and *that* was going to be a problem for me, a battle I had to prepare myself for. There was no living being or organization on this planet that would keep my wife away from me for a week, let alone two months, without being able to speak.

"I understand," I said because I did. "We need to talk about that but first..."

I nudged her back and immersed myself between her thighs again, sucking and licking her clit with my tongue simultaneously. I drove my fingers into her over and over again, grazing her g-spot each time.

She writhed beneath me, rolling her hips and begging for me to let her cum. I applied more pressure, grazing my teeth against her sensitive nub.

"Fuck you," she cried, tensing and then jerking forward, her body finally catching that high.

"Good girl."

I continued to devour her, sliding my fingers in and out while she made a mess all over my face—a perfect fucking mess. She fell back, her joined wrists above her head and body slack. I dragged my tongue up her pussy one last time, collecting her juices and savoring the taste before pulling away.

"I hate you."

I smirked and removed my pants.

After I settled between her thighs, my dick standing at attention, I undid the belt that she could've easily gotten out of but chose to keep on.

"We both know you don't mean that," I mused, removing the pins that were keeping her hair up until it was loose and spread out on the bed. "That's better."

I leaned forward and wrapped my lips around her nipple, suckling the small bud softly. Lucia gave me a little pleasured moan and wrapped her arms around my neck. She spread her legs for me, hooking one around my waist and resting the other between mine.

I kept sucking, moving from one to the other, giving them both equal attention. My dick had a mind of its own, jerking up and then dropping right on top of her bare mound. I needed to be inside of this woman, *stat!* I pressed Lucia down further into the mattress, giving her some of my body weight.

Hooking my arms under her, I slid into her. The way she sucked me in, welcoming me back to a place I'd found solace once before, gave me pause. I took a moment to stare into her eyes. She was... *something else.*

"You can't look at me like that," she said, her tone soft and far away.

"Like what?" I asked, removing myself and then thrusting forward.

I kept it slow, slower than it had been before. Lucia whimpered, her eyes closed and mouth agape.

"Look at me."

She obliged, her gaze filled with an expression I knew all too well.

"How do I look at you?"

"Like..." she gasped as I dove in deeper. "like you see me."

I dropped my forehead to hers, pressing my lips into her mouth and kissing the fuck out of her. She was eager to return the passion, lifting her hips to meet my quickened strokes. Lucia moaned melodiously into my mouth, her breathing picking up after I found the right angle to fuck her in. I drove into her, again and again, losing myself in the sensation washing over me.

"Don't hold back. Let me hear you moan, baby."

Her fingers scraped my neck as she brought them up to cup the back of my head. The tips of her nails dug into my scalp, and the slight pain jolted me forward, just as she'd wanted. I fucked her like my life depended on getting us off, slipping and sliding in and out of her pussy.

I buried my face into her neck and sank my teeth into her flesh.

"Yes," she cried into my ear, the sting from her nails growing more intense. "More..."

I bit down harder and soothed the spot with a long swipe of my tongue while plunging deep. Her back arched, and I whispered, "Cum for me, Scarlet."

"Enzo..."

I'd barely heard her, the breathy sound a mere whisper against my skin as she came. Her pussy tightened around my dick, and I let out a strangled growl, my strokes turning erratic as my own release pushed me over the edge.

"Through the shutters and shadows," I whispered against

her ear through our panted breaths. "I see you. You can't hide the rest forever."

She clung to me but never responded, something I hadn't expected her to do.

It didn't matter that we were married and had a connection; neither of us knew enough about the other person to go all in. And because I understood, I kissed her lips and got up to grab a warm washcloth from the en suite bathroom.

A few moments later, I stepped back into the room to find her sitting at the edge of the bed, her pistol in her hand. She looked at me, conflicted.

"You thinking about shooting me?" I asked, walking toward her with the rag in hand. "Or am I allowed to touch you still?"

Her lips twitched, and then she set it aside, laying back and opening for me.

"If I were going to kill you, it would be after you cleaned me up," she mused, sucking in a deep breath after I pressed the cloth into her sensitive area.

I moved the rag and kissed her pussy.

"Thanks for the heads up."

When I returned from disposing of the washcloth, she blurted some shit I hadn't expected but should've seen coming.

"I'm the one who shot Pietro."

This fucking woman.

It had never crossed my mind that a Red could actually be the shooter. Not even when my father informed me of the rumblings from our eyes and ears on the street. I still believed the Costas were using it as a way to downplay them not having answers while somehow being closer to the truth than they know.

"I could've used a nap before you told me that shit, Lucia."

"I'm only telling you because it might be something that

affects you later..." she twirled her ring and then said, "Now that we're married and all."

"Is that what you've been off doing?"

She frowned and grabbed my button-up, pushing her arms through and then clasping a few of them to cover herself.

"I was working."

"A job you failed to tell me about."

She shot an evil glare in my direction that did nothing. Even after drowning in her slick walls, I was still worked up about Giovanni, and now she was dropping this shit on me. I felt like testing out how mad I could make her with my questions.

"Because it was none of your fucking business," she snapped, standing and attempting to walk away.

"*You* are my fucking business," I retorted, grabbing her arm and dragging her body into mine. "More now than ever."

She snatched her arm from my hold but stayed in place, her wary gaze staring into mine.

"The keyword is *now*. I'll give you that, but I wasn't obligated to tell anything beforehand."

The irrational man I seemed to become around her didn't care about her being right. She didn't have to tell me shit at that time, but she *should* have after agreeing to marry me. I opened my mouth to say just that, but a crashing sound coming from the bottom level caught both of our attention. Lucia jumped into action, her tearing through the room for something to throw on while I grabbed my pants and dragged them onto my body.

I picked up my gun from the dresser and checked the clip just as she emerged from the walk-in closet in a pair of sweats and my shirt tied in a knot around her stomach. The second she grabbed her gun from the bed, I heard heavy footsteps and then a recognizable voice on the other side of the bedroom door.

"Bossman," Rocco called, his deep voice carrying through the wood. "This is um... probably a bad time, but I was the only one with enough balls to come here. You know, with Matteo and Malik being occupied and all."

I snatched the door open and stared at my enforcer and friend.

"Fuck did you break down there?"

"Oh..." he grinned mischievously. "That was just to warn you both that I was here." He leaned over to get a look at Lucia, the same as he had nine months ago at the casino. "I'll replace the cups."

She let out a breathless chuckle that I felt in my chest.

"They aren't mine, but if you don't want to hear Jaz's mouth, you might want to do it before she realizes it."

He nodded and turned his attention back to me, the expression in his eyes tense.

"Your father sent me..."

He paused, and I felt my patience weaning. I didn't have time for Rocco's dramatic way of delivering information. It worked my last nerve on a normal day, but right now it was pissing me the fuck off.

I sighed and rubbed the gun I was still holding against my forehead.

"Get to the point, Roc."

"You two have been summoned by your fathers."

Lucia laughed, and I stared at him in disbelief.

"They sent you here for that?"

"Hence why no one else wanted to come and interrupt..." he pointed to my bare chest.

"And using a phone didn't feel sufficient enough for either of them?"

Rocco's lips curled knowingly.

"They tried."

Lucia's laughter burst out of her again, and I turned to see what the fuck could be so funny.

"We're in trouble," she said, her eyes wide with amusement. "You killed a man in front of everyone. I embarrassed a mafia boss, and then we left our families with the mess."

Nothing about that shit was funny, but I found myself laughing with her.

"Roc, tell my father and Lucia's that they can *deal* with us later."

I slammed the door in his face, my mind on something much more appealing than having a sit down with our fathers like a couple of teenagers. I might've answered to mine for the time being, but I moved when I fucking felt like it. *Always.*

Chapter 15

Lucia

I drowned out the deep roar of my father's voice.

He was not pleased with me.

But what did he expect me to do? Stand there and allow myself to be physically abused by a man who knew nothing of me? Everyone should've been grateful I stopped Enzo from starting a war on our territory.

Now I had my father upset with me.

My mother was currently shouting orders at the gardeners while they cut and replaced the part of the lawn Giovanni's guard had been laid out on. It was an intense environment, what I'd walked into. And Luca was nowhere in sight, so I didn't have the backup I was used to.

"Lucia Gabriella Moretti!"

I blinked in his direction.

"Bianchi," I corrected, earning myself a look that could kill.

"You think this is a joke?" he asked, staring at me as if I'd lost my mind.

And maybe I had because I did find it funny that I was

being yelled at like a fourteen-year-old who'd just been caught skipping school.

"You have to admit that it is a little funny."

"Damnit, Lucia..." he hit the desk, and I frowned. "You need to think before you react."

"I did all the thinking I could with his grubby fingers digging into my ribs on *my* wedding day! He deserved to die, and I stopped that from happening."

I balled my fist up in my lap, piercing my flesh with the tips of my nails.

My father knew how much I hated being yelled at.

It drove me up a wall and sparked a different type of anger inside my body. When I'd been recruited into the Society, we were sent off to a boarding school. We endured things no person should have to, like being talked down on, yelled at, or beaten into submission. There were bruises to prove it. Some of us wore them like a badge of honor; I chose to cover mine with tattoos.

"If you'd been listening, you would know why I'm upset..." he sat back, the furrow in his brows loosening. "Are you done zoning out on me?"

"If you're done yelling at me, yes."

"As a woman in your position," he started, ignoring my snark. "What would you do to someone that defied your trust? Went against the code and not only embarrassed you but caused harm to your bottom line?"

"I would put a bullet in their head," I answered without pause and then said, "I get it. I'm not stupid."

"I never said you were, Luci. In fact, I think you're smarter than a lot of the men I deal with on a daily. But you're not alone in this anymore. There are other people who will pay the cost for your actions. Enzo may agree with you, but his father is still the boss. Remember, your moves affect him the most."

I sighed, knowing he was right, but annoyed by it at the same time.

Maybe marrying Enzo had been a mistake. Not only had I put myself in a shaky situation when it came to my responsibilities to the Society, but I had to move differently as well. All of the things I'd feared but somehow forgot about in the heat of the moment.

"I don't know how to do this..." I looked into my father's eyes, hoping he could give me clarity—advice. "Be a wife and think of others before myself."

"No?" he leaned forward and pulled something from his desk drawer. "You think of two people every time you move."

The folder he slid my way had more information than even I knew about Jaz and Violet. I scanned the pages, but as the guilt settled in, I slammed it shut and slid it back.

"They're different."

"Are they? Or is it because of the way they'd come into your life?"

I shook my head.

"You know too much, *padre*."

"I know more than you think I do, *Figlia*." He stashed the folder and rested his arms on the desk, gaze on me—*reading me*. "The things you've been up to. The people you've been dragging into it. I know all and see all when it comes to my children. What I don't understand is why it's so important to you."

I felt frozen in place like my plans were crumbling before I even got started. He wasn't asking me to stop, but I'd rather he'd been doing that instead of asking me the purpose of it all. The answer would set him ablaze. Luca, too.

"I just want to do a little good," I said, finding the strength to look him in the eyes again. "With all that you do, all the things you're into, do you ever feel that you have to do some good in order to level the playing field?"

"No."

"Never?"

"Never."

I nodded.

"I see—"

"But I give back because it comes naturally to me. Not because I see myself as a man wanting to right his wrongs. I'm not doing anything other than living in my truth. There is no clear-cut definition of what's considered to be good or bad, Lucia. There are evil people in this world. And then there are people like us."

I had so many things I wanted to say, so many thoughts and feelings about 'living in our truth,' but I kept them to myself. Because my truth—no matter how it felt deep down inside— was never wanting to be anyone other than the person I'd become.

"I'm sorry that mom's in a frenzy."

He laughed.

"She'll be fine..." he slid a phone across the desk. "Joaquin left this for you. Break's over."

I stared at the new burner, identical to the one I'd thrown into the Atlantic a week ago. Picking up the small device, I powered it on, and one encrypted message rolled in, and I punched in my unique code to reveal the request. I eyed the screen closely.

Target: Rex Benton

Last known location: Newark, New Jersey

Pay: $1,000,000

Time frame: One week

The picture of a man with a deranged glint in his eyes popped up next.

His lips were curved into a daring smirk, and I was up for that challenge.

"Was it really a break?" I asked, accepting the contract. "Feels like I never stopped working."

I stood and stuffed the phone into my pocket after powering it off again.

"Your brother is at the restaurant," he informed me. "See him before you leave the city."

I nodded and turned.

"Hey, Dad," I called, stopping at the door and glancing over my shoulder. "You'll call if you need me, right?"

He chuckled, his midnight black irises sparkling a little.

It was a serious question. I loved my family, and even though I was only moving an hour away, it felt like I was giving up more than just distance and time.

"Luci, if I need you, I'll do you one better and hire you."

I nodded and left, heading out into the gardens that were now cleared from yesterday's mess of a *wedding*. My mother spotted me instantly and made her way over.

"You promised me no blood."

I pulled her into a tight embrace.

"I know, and I'm sorry. How can I make it up to you?"

I hated seeing her in a rage.

"Grandkids," she murmured into my neck. "You can make it up to me by bringing me grandchildren to tend to."

I rolled my eyes to the sky and then pulled away, holding onto her arms.

"I'll see what I can do about that in about a year or two."

She balked, and I laughed, backing away before she could lecture me about family and procreation. I loved my mother, but she was a lot to deal with at times, especially when talking about marriage and children.

"I love you, and I'll see you soon, okay?"

"I'm never going to see you again," she said, sighing. "I

barely saw you when you lived twenty minutes away. Now you'll be an hour away and in another state."

I paused, taken aback by the sadness in her voice.

"Ma..." I stepped forward, and she shook her head, stopping me in my tracks. "I knew you and Luca would grow up and live your own lives, but I never foresaw this. I'm proud of you, you know? For being as fierce as I'd prayed for you to be."

"I know you are. I'll do better. How about dinner twice a month? We can share the responsibility of bringing everyone together."

She nodded, but I somehow knew she didn't believe I'd do it.

My life was hectic, but I'd been living it the same way since I was seventeen years old. I had no clue the toll it would take on my mother, and that bothered me. Was I really the daughter she'd hoped for?

"I love you," I called as she turned.

"I love you more, baby girl. Go be a wife and a..."

Her voice trailed, but we both knew where her mind had gone, and I left. My heart ached all the way to my next destination. Luca noticed the moment I walked into MoreSoul, one of our three Soulfood restaurants in the Tri-state, that something was bothering me.

The space had a diner feel to it but more modern with its large dark-colored booths, oak tables with slight marbling to them, and low-hanging light fixtures over each. The dining room was packed, and all eyes shifted upon my entry, staying glued to me as I passed each to get to my brother.

"What's wrong?" he asked after I slid into the booth he occupied at the back of the restaurant.

It was private enough that he could conduct business without people overhearing but positioned where he could watch the room.

"Does ma seem sad to you?"

He shook his head, eyes scanning the floor once more before settling on me again.

"She wasn't ready to see you married off, contrary to the lectures we get about children."

"Why didn't I know that?"

He gave me a look that said I should know the answer, and I did, but I was having a hard time coming to terms with it.

"Don't get worked up about it. She'll adjust, same as always..." Luca leaned forward, his gaze—the same as our father's—penetrating through me in only a way he could. "You and Enzo knew one another this entire time, didn't you?"

I tossed him a guilty smile.

"Not for long."

"But long enough that you're now his wife?"

I shook my head.

"Not necessarily. It's a long story."

"You could have come to me if you're in trouble, Luci."

His voice broke a little.

Fuck me.

He was hurt or offended, maybe a little concerned, and now I had another person who meant the world to me, disappointed in my actions. Luca and I were more than just twins, he was my best friend, but I couldn't always tell him what was going on. He had enough on his plate as is.

"I'm not in trouble. I would never keep that from you."

We stared at one another for a while, but eventually, I got a nod of understanding.

"I know Dad sent me here for a reason, so what's up?"

"I want to expand," he said, waving his hand. "The restaurants are doing good, and we need to capitalize on it."

And I had to agree because of my stake in it.

The restaurants had always been more Luca's thing than

mine. It was the first task our father assigned him to tackle after becoming made. We'd gone from a small mom-and-pop feel to franchise worthy in a short time because of him.

"Whatever you want to do, you have my vote."

His lips tilted up.

"So, you'll have my back when I propose putting one inside of the Myriad."

I chuckled and leaned back, crossing my arms.

"You'd have to at least be cordial with the man before proposing business."

"I know how to be a civilized human being."

"Mmhm, sure you do, brother."

Dante slid into the booth beside me, a plate I knew he'd gotten straight from the kitchen in hand. He forked a large portion of mac and cheese and stuffed it into his mouth before speaking.

"Did you ask her?" he asked, completely ignoring my existence.

Dante was my idea of a smooth-talking Italian man through and through. He had eyes the color of the ocean, the clearest blue I'd ever seen on a man with lashes longer than my extensions, and that signature olive skin. Tall and lanky but always eating was Dante Cardona.

"I'm sitting right here, Dante."

He continued to eat without addressing me.

I hooked a thumb in his direction while staring at Luca.

"Don't tell me he's mad at me, too."

"He's just upset that you gave your condo to Violet and Jaz."

Dante was more like family than anything. He'd grown up in foster care, never knowing his real family until later in life. A scholarship landed him at our private school, and the rest, as they say, is history. He and Luca were inseparable, and that turned into them becoming made men around the same time. I trusted him with my life and my brother's.

"He has..." I turned from Luca and took Dante's plate and fork, stuffing greens into my mouth and then sliding it back. "You have the funds to buy your own place."

"Too much work," he said, sharing a piece of catfish with me—a peace offering.

I bumped his shoulder and chuckled.

"Hire someone, Ugly."

Then, I reached into the pocket of my jacket and laid a single key between us on the table. He cut his gaze at it and then at me.

"The one next door is all yours. It went on the market, and I bought it on a whim. My plans were to open it up and combine the spaces, but I have no need for it now. Besides, I need someone to keep a close eye on Jaz and Violet."

"We weren't going to forget about them," Luca said, looking at something behind us.

Dante turned, but I didn't need to.

I felt him.

Like always, my skin burned but prickled with goosebumps. My heart raced in recognition and anticipation. It was too much. I couldn't take it.

But I wanted to.

So *fucking* bad.

Enzo appeared, and I looked around for Malik or Matteo to avoid his penetrating gaze. I'd left him this morning without saying anything, but it hadn't been on purpose. I was used to moving and not telling others my whereabouts. By the time I'd realized what I'd done, it was too late, and I decided to keep on with my day.

"Sit," Luca offered, forcing me to face my *husband*.

He stared at me and then at Dante, who hadn't made an

attempt to move. I elbowed him in the ribs, and he hissed.

"What the fuck, Lucia," Dante grumbled, gripping his side.

Enzo raised an eyebrow.

"If you don't move so Enzo can sit, I'll break them one by one, D."

Because he knew I would do it, Dante slid out and next to Luca.

Enzo didn't move to sit, and I fought not to roll my eyes.

"Luca has something he wants to talk to you about..." I slanted a look in my brother's direction. "...I think you might be interested."

I'd piqued his curiosity enough that he obliged Luca's offer to sit, sliding in so close our arms were pressed tightly together. The smell of cedarwood filled my nostrils, and I just barely stopped myself from sighing in contentment. He brushed his fingers up against my thigh, squeezed, and then rested them there.

I rolled my bottom lip between my teeth and stared at the table, refusing to look Luca and Dante in the eyes. They *could not* see me like this, in awe of a man.

"Moretti," Enzo spoke, inclining his head. "We need to make this quick."

"Do you like Soulfood?" Dante blurted, forcing me to look at him. "You grew up in a big Italian family. Fresh pasta and sauce. Basil from a garden, never from the store. Is that more your thing? I didn't know shit about Italian food until I met these two. Soul food is more my thing now."

Enzo leaned back, his fingers flexing against my knee.

"A little bit of both," he replied, surprising me. "Those homemade dishes are a luxury I don't get often anymore."

My heart staggered a little at that.

What did that mean?

I'd thought Enzo's grandmother was still in his life or that his own mother would be making those signature dishes you get when in an Italian family. My nonna on my dad's side loved to cook big feasts when I was a young girl. She'd have the entire estate smelling like fresh herbs and spices every day. I remember her teaching my mother how to make her most prized recipes, and then my mother taught me after nonna passed. She was the sweetest being I'd ever known, and I missed her dearly.

I placed my hand on top of Enzo's and slid my fingers through his.

"We're thinking of expanding," Luca cut in. "What do you think about opening a MoreSoul in the Myriad?"

Enzo surprised me when he brought our joined fingers to his mouth, softly kissing the back of my hand. He brushed his lips over my knuckles and then said, "I'll put you in touch with my general manager. Work the rest out with your sister. Anything else?"

"Yeah..." Luca paused, his gaze shifting to the left. "Senator Michaels, to what do we owe the pleasure?"

The energy at the table shifted at the mention of the New Jersey state senator. He had a habit of being in the same places as us more often than not lately.

"My wife is obsessed with the mac and cheese this place serves up. I thought I'd stop in on my way back to New Jersey and order her some to go."

It was the worst excuse and outright comical.

"Nice suit," Enzo mused, his lips curving into an amused smile. "Seems a little out of your budget but nice, nonetheless."

The man was dressed in a custom Brioni; I knew that stitching anywhere.

Senator Michaels glared down at us, his eyes briefly pausing on our joined fingers.

"Ah..." Enzo lifted our hands after noticing where his attention had gone. "We got married yesterday."

"Congratulations."

He cut his gaze over to Luca, who sat eerily quiet.

"I better get going," he said. "I only wanted to stop over and praise the good work. I hope you can keep up the momentum." He chuckled and shook his head. "You must love this place."

The senator walked away, leaving his veiled threat hanging in the air.

"Don't worry about that," Enzo said, sliding out of the booth and taking me with him. "He's a little grumpy about a dinner I crashed some months back. I'll keep the senator out of your business."

From the look on my brother's face, I had a feeling that the Senator hadn't shown up here in retaliation to what happened in D.C. That made me wonder what Luca had been up to while I was away.

"I'll check in soon," I called out when Enzo started walking away, my hand still in his. "Keep an eye on Jaz and Violet. I love you."

"Always and forever," he called back.

We made it out of MoreSoul, and Enzo turned to me, smashing his lips against mine. We engaged in a kiss so passionate my knees barely stood a chance. I felt it deep inside of me, taking root and staking its claim. Enzo tersely pulled away and gripped my chin.

"The next time you leave me without a proper goodbye, we'll have a big fucking problem, Lucia."

He dragged me into him again, kissed me hard, and then ushered me over to the waiting truck—Malik at the wheel. My lips tingled with awareness, and I paused before climbing inside, glancing into his eyes over my shoulder.

"I want to be kissed like that when you aren't mad at me."

Just like that. Always like that.

Chapter 16

Enzo

I watched her from my private suite.
Dressed in a form-fitting black mini dress, her hair straightened and hanging down her back. The heels on her feet were sky-high, the only way she wore them. I couldn't look away. No matter how pissed I was, I couldn't find it in me to step in.

I wasn't sure if it was out of respect or intrigue, maybe both.

But seeing Lucia on the prowl turned me the fuck on.

"Here's your drink, Mr. Bianchi."

The waitress set the three fingers of Cognac down on the small table beside me and excused herself after I handed over a hundred-dollar tip. I picked up the glass and sipped, my eyes scanning the lowly lit strip club, Obsidian.

There were three stages, all of them occupied by dancers.

The room had a mixture of booths and tables, all full.

Bottle girls pranced around, dancers crowded one table in particular.

Obsidian sat in my territory.

Lucia was on the job in *my* territory.

We'd only seen one another in passing over the last few days. Living together did nothing for the craving I had of wanting to see her every second of every minute. It was driving me fucking insane, and everyone around me sensed it.

"Who's the target, *Bellissima*?" I murmured, following her frame to a table near the back.

There was another body sitting in the darkened corner, turned away from me and not easily identifiable. I flexed my fingers around the glass and watched them interact with rapt attention.

For a brief moment, Lucia paused and shifted her attention to the suite I occupied. The glass was tinted enough that I knew she couldn't see me, but that didn't mean she couldn't *feel* me. And the thought of that made my dick hard.

I'm here, baby.

She looked away, said a few more words, and then got up—ducking behind a curtain to the right of them. The man she'd been talking to stood and followed, and then I was on the move, leaving the privacy of my suite in search of where they'd gone.

I moved down a corridor and a flight of stairs. On the lower level, there were three rooms. I checked the first two and paused outside of the third. With my gun drawn, I listened but quickly learned that it was soundproof.

"Hey, what are you—"

"Your job isn't to worry about me," I said, pointing my gun at the head of my server. "Move."

She hurried off, and I slipped quietly into the room.

It was lowly lit, just like the main floor. Red suede upholstery draped the entire interior, from the curtains down to the carpet and sofas. I kept to the shadows, my back against the wall near the door, covered by thick drapery.

Lucia's voice was soft, barely above a whisper.

"What did you do that warranted a visit from me?"

A muffled sound and then a manic chuckle came next. I leaned slightly to the left to get a look at them. She was standing straight, her back to me. This man, just like the last, was barely visible enough to identify.

"Sorry," she said. "I forgot I requested a gag..." that once muffled sound turned into a low plea.

"Please. I-I don't know what I did."

Lucia *tsked*.

"I don't believe you. I wouldn't be here if you were innocent, Rex. Tell me what you did, and I won't make you suffer."

"T-They think I killed one of them," he confessed, the words spilling from his lips quicker than I expected. "I didn't touch that girl. She was fucking crazy."

"What girl?"

"Mariana Costa."

She hummed, her interest piqued as was mine.

"Tell me more."

"She disappeared soon after Pietro Junior was shot. Everyone knows it's connected. They thought she did it, but then her body was delivered right to their doorstep. I was the last one to see her alive."

"Sounds like you know more than you're letting on..." she tipped her head in question. "...or maybe not. Seeing as I was the last one to see her alive."

"You..."

Lucia chuckled and flipped her hair off her shoulder. She moved to the side, and I was able to see the man I now knew as Rex. His hands and feet were tied.

"I'm sorry you got dragged into this," she said, almost actually sounding remorseful. "Sometimes, there are casualties in war. I also apologize that I can't let you go."

"There has to be something you want to know. I-I'll tell you everything."

"You're a low-level soldier with a target on his back. Why should I believe you know anything worth hearing?"

"People talk. I listen. You never know how useful information can be until someone comes looking for it."

Disgusted, I made my presence known.

Rex's eyes widened as I stepped further into the dim light. Lucia, on the other hand, didn't acknowledge me right away. I'd sensed when I entered that she knew I was there.

"Don't worry about him, Rex," she said, confirming my suspicions. "He's upset I haven't made it home for dinner three nights in a row."

"Three nights is a lot, don't you think, Rex?" I asked, eyes on him. "Especially for a pair of newlyweds."

Rex looked perplexed as he shifted his attention between the two of us.

"I know you," he blurted. "Enzo Bianchi."

His gaze whipped to Lucia, his mouth agape.

"Moretti..."

The stench of his fear became more pungent.

"Bianchi," I corrected. "Married, remember?"

"Maybe you guys should work on that and let me go," he posed, still looking for a way out. "I'll be long gone by the time I'm even a thought in your head again."

"No can do, Rexford."

Rexford?

The fuck kind of name is Rexford?

"But you can help me fix my husband's attitude by telling me what I want to hear and then taking this..." she lifted a needle filled halfway. "...a single pump into a vein should do the job quickly."

"Or I can take my anger out on you with a few bullets to the gut. Worse pain you'll ever feel, trust me." I pointed my gun at him. "What do you say? Tell the lady what she wants to hear, so I can take her home."

She cut her eyes in my direction, a form of acknowledgment I'd accept for the time being. But she would pay.

"People aren't allowed to speak the last name Moretti on Costa territory," he revealed. "It's a death sentence."

"Is that all?" Lucia asked, annoyance clear in her tone. "I could give two fucks about being the Voldemort of the mafia. An ego boost maybe, but nothing else worth writing home about."

"Voldemort?" I asked, brows raised.

"Don't judge my love for Harry Potter. Now isn't the time, Bianchi."

I smiled.

"Rex, I'm getting impatient here," I said. "Maybe if I—"

"N-N-No..." he looked at me. "They're out to sabotage and then take over."

"Tell me something I don't know..." Lucia placed a knee on the wall-length bench and gripped his chin. "Or do you not have the valuable information you claimed to know?"

"Senior and Junior are fighting a lot. They're at odds and it's spilling over into business, especially after Junior was shot."

I wasn't satisfied with this information, so I popped the safety on my gun for emphasis.

"Senior wants your father dead!" he yelled, taking the hint.

She stilled, her hand holding the needle directly behind his earlobe.

"He's been making moves on their territory. Stealing transports and infiltrating their docks. They're losing money and patience. We're on high alert. There's more security everywhere."

"Thanks, Rex..." she jabbed the needle into his neck and

released whatever was inside into him. "You've been a big help."

He struggled, writhing against her for a few seconds until his body turned rigid. His eyes were wide and still moving.

"It paralyzes first," she told me, standing. "And then his organs stop working one by one. He'll be dead in less than a minute."

Lucia turned to me, her gaze dancing.

"You shouldn't have come here."

"A little too late for that, don't you think?"

She looked away from me and checked Rex's pulse.

A low satisfied hum filled the space around us, and I tucked my gun away.

"He lied," she said, turning to face me. "About them upping security. They've got all hands on deck at the Costa estate. The docks are shut down. No transports had been coming in and out until Monroe called about one tonight."

"Who are you sending?"

She sighed.

"Violet and Jaz and one other person."

I raised an eyebrow.

"You don't know him but he's trustworthy."

I took her hand, and we exited the room together.

The club was packed still as we maneuvered through. Once we made it out into the chilly night, she turned and wrapped her arms around my torso. I couldn't do shit but return the affection because I missed her.

"Don't pull your gun on him," she whispered just before pulling away.

"Look at you, Scarlet," a deep voice teased, stepping from the side of the building but staying in the shadows. "Last I checked, you hated being touched."

He was tall and dressed in black but unmistakably didn't

want to be seen.

I wasn't fucking with that. Not being able to identify someone standing in the same vicinity as me—as my wife.

"Don't be weird, Mekhi," she said, turning to face him but keeping her body up against mine. "Thank you for the intel."

"Anything for you."

She rested the back of her head on my chest, and I draped an arm around her, pulling her body closer. I didn't trust easily, but her relaxed demeanor kept me complacent.

"I owe you for just now and later."

Ah.

He was the third person.

"You know what I want. Make it happen, and we'll be even."

He disappeared from view, and she said, "He's shy."

"I want to take you somewhere," I replied, not giving a fuck about her friend. "Up for a ride?"

She turned, removing herself from my embrace.

"The last time you asked me to take a ride with you, we ended up on a jet."

Malik pulled up to the curb, and I took her hand, leading us over to the truck.

"We're staying local this time."

I helped her into the back and got in behind her.

"Hey, Malik," she greeted, leaning between the seats. "Are we really staying local?"

"We are," he answered, surprising me.

Lucia sat back and pulled her seatbelt on, tucking the strap behind her back.

"Fine..." she wiggled her feet. "...but I'm taking these off."

Malik started us on our short journey, and I reached for her leg, bringing it into my lap and removing the heel. I held my hand out for the other, and she twisted to give me access.

"Harry Potter?" I questioned, kneading the sole of her foot.

"What?" she pulled her bottom lip between her teeth. "A girl can't enjoy books?"

Her parents' home had a bookcase in almost every room. It made sense that she would like to read. I found it a little sexy, too.

"Why does one room have fake books?"

"It moves..." She cut her eyes at me. "The shelf. You can get to any room in the house from that one."

I figured it was something along those lines.

"Where are we—"

Malik pulled to a stop outside of my parent's brownstone.

"Dinner with the family."

Lucia looked down at herself and then at me with a deep frown on her pretty face.

"I'm not dressed for a casual dinner."

Malik handed me the pair of black and white Jordan ones I'd pulled from her closet before leaving the apartment. I took the socks I'd stuffed into the left shoe and slipped them onto her feet before helping her into the high tops.

"No, but you do look dressed to kill," I mused, opening my door with a smirk on my face.

"Ha. Ha. "You're lucky I'm starving."

"You're lucky I don't take you home and fuck you until hunger pains set in." I shut the backdoor and waved for Malik to lower the window. "Park and come inside or take a break. Your choice. We're good here."

He nodded and pulled off, and I led us inside, where we were met by Gianna whispering into her phone. After spotting us, she hung up and pasted on a smile.

"Look who has arrived. The prince and princess themselves."

She bowed and curtsied.

"Takes a princess to know one," Lucia said, chuckling—not in the least bit offended by my sister's sass. "He wouldn't understand."

Gianna—who I was used to having an attitude about life in general—smiled genuinely.

"They never do. Glad to have someone who does around for a change."

She spun on her heels and headed toward the dining room. Lucia moved to follow, but I stopped her, keeping us in the corridor.

"What don't I know about my sister?"

My mind was on that first encounter we shared.

"Your sister is not who you think she is."

I knew Gia was a spitfire, but I was beginning to believe I needed to pay closer attention to her and the moves she was making.

"I can see the wheels in your head turning," Lucia said, brushing her fingers up against my chest. "Whatever you do, don't be the overbearing brother who goes searching for answers he isn't ready to hear yet."

That response only heightened my intrigue.

"She's finding her way," she added. "We all have to."

I tucked my hand under her chin, tilting her head back slightly.

"I still don't know what to do with you."

"I don't know, *marito*—husband..." her lips curled. "I think you know exactly what to do with me... *to* me."

Instead of responding by dragging her back home, I kissed her.

Soft and slow, nipping at her bottom lip until she whimpered.

"Now, let's go eat."

I walked away, satisfied that she was as flustered as I was.

Chapter 17

Lucia

"Nice sneakers," Rocco complimented as he swaggered past me with a plate of pasta, four large meatballs, and two pieces of garlic bread. "Can't stay."

My stomach rumbled a little, reminding me that I hadn't eaten in hours.

"If I asked a favor, would you do it?" I inquired, pausing his pursuit to the front door.

Rocco turned, his lips pulled into an easy smile.

His laid-back personality was more genuine than Matteo's. The man looked to have no worries in the world but was as deadly as they come. I was certain I'd get to see him in action soon enough.

"Depends on what this favor entails."

"Just a little surveillance." I shrugged. "I know you're busy, but I'm sure you have a man to spare. One that you trust with sensitive information."

He regarded me with keen eyes, the plate in his hands lowering enough for me to notice.

"How close to the chest am I keeping it?"

"So, close that no man with the last name Bianchi can know."

He nodded slowly, overthinking how he wanted to play it. What I was asking of him was against code. His moves belonged to the Bianchi family. Where he went, who he spoke to, down the bodies he bagged. There were no side jobs. No secrets kept close to the chest. None of it. But I had a good feeling about Rocco and his judgment.

"Is that a yes?" I asked, unlocking my phone.

"When I learn what it is, I have the option to walk away. No harm, no foul."

I pulled up the number I needed on my phone and then turned it around so he could see.

"Call this number. Hear her out and make your choice."

Rocco stared at my phone's screen for all of a few seconds before nodding and walking away. I was confident in my decision to choose him.

"I saw you before," Gianna said from behind me.

I turned to find her leaning against the archway that led into the front room.

Gianna was print model gorgeous. With her deep brown skin and large doe ravened colored eyes. She was all legs and athletically thin, her dips and curves more defined.

"Oh yeah?" I walked past her, and she fell into step with me. "What did you see before?"

"You at the casino," she revealed. "Months ago. You and Enzo were talking. I thought I recognized you, but I hadn't been sure."

"I saw you, too," I told her, smiling as we paused in the living room. "I also saw—"

Her eyes widened, and she shushed me while glancing

toward the kitchen where the bass of her father and brother's voices carried.

"Please don't tell Enzo."

She feared his reaction—his disappointment, not him.

I had a feeling the two Bianchi brothers were closer to their sister than they let on.

"Your secret is safe with me..." I held up my pinkie, and she rolled her eyes but latched on. "Now we're best friends. Have my back, and I'll have yours."

She smirked.

"I won't tell Enzo about your little deal with Rocco. As long as you don't plan on hurting my brother or family in any way."

"Is that a threat, Ms. Bianchi?"

"A promise."

I smiled.

"You and I are going to get along fine."

Gianna Bianchi was *just my* type of girl.

"I don't know if I like the idea of you two becoming close," Matteo said as we entered the kitchen through the dining room. "Gut feeling."

"Always go with your gut, brother," Gianna said, bumping into him on purpose as she passed. "Isn't that what you tell me?"

She smiled sweetly in his direction, earning a chuckle from Enzo.

"At least we know you retain some information."

"I retain what's useful. Can we eat now?"

Emilia came sauntering out of the kitchen with a pitcher of something dark purple in color. She set it down and then took her seat adjacent to Angelo's spot at the head of the table. Enzo sat across from his mother, and I finally moved, taking the empty chair beside him.

Matteo sat next to Emilia, and Gia found herself next to me.

The table was long enough to fit about six more people, and with just us, it felt... *empty*—like something was missing.

"One of you, be sure to take Brandon a plate on your way back," Emilia said after grace. "My sister would have a fit if she were alive and knew you had him working during our scheduled family dinners."

She cut her gaze between Enzo and Matteo.

"He makes the schedule," Matteo said, scoffing. "I'm starting to think Brandon likes it when we are made to deliver food to him."

Plates of fresh homemade pasta began to make their rounds; next came the vodka sauce and then meatballs. They were rolled perfectly and baked to perfection. The smell of basil wafted past me, and my nonna came to mind, and then my mother.

"I'll take it to him," Gianna offered.

When plates were filled, the talking stopped.

This was my first time having dinner with them. It felt awkward and forced, almost like they were recreating what they had before removing themselves from the *other* Bianchi fold.

It became too quiet.

I was used to bickering with Dante. Or listening to Luca talk about some new business idea. It didn't matter if it was my mother going on and on about her charities or my father silently listening to everyone's conversations; there was always something happening.

Don't even get me started about when Gaia and her mom attend. Toss in Violet and Jaz, and chaos is guaranteed.

Though I didn't get to attend all of those family dinners, this simply didn't feel like one.

"Would you mind if I invited my family to a dinner sometime in the near future?" I asked, wanting to make good on my promise to my mom but also to give us something—anything, to talk about. "I think maybe my mom having a hard time with me being further away."

I hadn't meant to admit that or allow the sadness I felt about it to be heard, but from the look in Emilia's eyes, I had done just that. She almost looked to be apologetic. Almost as if she'd thought I'd been forced into this.

"Of course. I'd love to host them."

She nodded, affirming what she'd said and making me feel a tidbit more welcomed.

"Okay..."

My attempt to engage had backfired because now I was wondering if my mother had eaten. If she cooked anything for the family tonight. Was everyone too busy to sit down with her this week? Just once?

I looked down at my plate and began to eat, upset that I wasn't properly savoring how good Emilia's cooking was. With every delicious bite, I felt like a traitor.

Enzo's hand landed on my leg, and I glanced over to find him closely observing me. He slipped his fingers between my thighs and squeezed before I turned away. The man kept me turned on and keyed up without really trying.

"Did Enzo inform you of the Juliette Gala?" Angelo asked, sparking up some much-needed conversation.

"He mentioned it in passing," I said, wiping my hands and picking up the pitcher to pour myself something to drink. "What's the cause?"

I took a sip and reared back, staring at my glass as if it were a flashback from my childhood.

"It's a—"

"Grape Kool-Aid?" I questioned, cutting Angelo off. Realizing what I'd done, I lifted my gaze to meet his. "I apologize; it's just..." I shook my head. "Never mind. You were saying?"

He continued on like nothing had happened, but I couldn't focus; my mind had shut down and wasn't retaining anything being said.

The rest of the dinner passed by in the blink of an eye, and before I knew it, Enzo and I were saying goodbye and sliding into the back of the Escalade with Malik at the wheel. I was grateful for the silent ride home, but Enzo wasn't going for that when we entered the penthouse.

"Tell me," he started, taking me by the waist and lifting me onto the kitchen island. He parted my legs with his hand and slid between them. "What significance does grape Kool-Aid have in your life?"

I felt vulnerable all of a sudden, and my heart began to race.

The sick feeling I'd had at dinner came rushing back. Not because the memory was a bad one but because it would be another way in for him. Another way for Enzo to find a permanent place in my heart.

"It's silly..." I lowered my head, and he lifted it almost immediately.

"I want to know. Silly or not, I want to know everything about Luci."

I sighed, aware that I wouldn't put up a fight.

We were connected until death do us part, and I actually liked him.

Crazily enough, I trusted him, too; I believed he was on my side.

And I was on his.

"My grandmother didn't know she was mixed..." I wrapped my arms around his neck, needing a little support. Telling my grandmother's story broke my heart. "She was as white-passing as they come, her olive shading was a little deeper than most, but to the average eye, she was a full-blooded Italian."

I knew he knew the story.

Everyone knew the details of my nonna, and her family being disowned after learning of her parent's betrayal. The Moretti's were a low-status famiglia within the Costa ranks. My great-grandfather used his daughter as payment, forcing her into a marriage with Pietro Senior. He was a cruel man and did unthinkable things to her and those around him.

"And?" Enzo pushed, kissing my forehead and then resting his against it.

"After it was all said and done, my great-grandmother eventually told my grandmother about her father. Where he was and how to find him. She took that information, packed up my dad, and left for Chicago with the hopes that when she returned, she would understand who she truly was."

Enzo's lips grazed mine, and I went in for the kiss, needing to make up for the days we'd barely spent time together this week. I still didn't know how to balance my new life. I felt like a failure across the board.

"They got there, and their world changed," I whispered into his mouth. "She connected with her father, the family she'd never known. That turned into Chicago becoming home for them. Neither returned until my father learned the truth about himself and decided his fate. I guess it made sense to him why he felt drawn to a life of crime. By then, he'd met my mother, and she was too in love to let him leave without her."

I pulled back a little to look him in the eyes.

"I guess I said all of that to say that my grandmother would sneak me a cup of grape Kool-Aid every night until I was twelve. It was our thing. I hadn't drunk any since her passing."

"She passed after your twelfth birthday," he surmised, putting two and two together.

I nodded and released his neck, pushing my fingers into his shirt and dragging it up.

"Dinner felt weird. Was it my presence or..." I looked up at him. "...was it something else?"

I rested my hand over his heart, and he sighed, placing one of his atop it.

"It's all fucked up, Scarlet."

My insides whirred in pleasure at his use of my nickname. He had no idea at the time of hearing it from Monroe where I'd gotten it and how. But I was certain after finding out that I was a Red he understood.

"When you grow up with no less than fifteen people eating dinner together every night, and then one day it turns into five and stays that way..." He cupped my chin and brushed his thumb across my bottom lip. "I love my family, but it's an adjustment. Starting over."

"Did you feel... *accolto?*" Accepted.

"As accepted as a Black man can feel in a place where no one but the people who shared the same DNA as him looked like him. The truth had been easy to ignore until it wasn't any longer. I didn't realize how much of a threat we were to them until I was old enough to understand why."

I felt for him—for the way they'd been treated.

Our stories were so different but somehow the same.

His father—a Black man through and through—had been raised by a predominantly Italian family. While my father—a biracial man—had been raised by his bi-racial mother and the Black side of her family.

"Your grandmother..."

"She's doing what's best for her," he said, angling my head back to kiss my neck. "Same as we are."

I admired them even more for knowing that it was okay to

remove themselves from the lives of people who didn't see their true worth. They were resilient—*he* was resilient.

"I want you," I whispered, hooking one leg around his waist and scraping my fingernails down his chest. "We've missed one another these last few days."

More like he came in while I was sleeping, and I left before he was awake. We wouldn't be able to live like that long before it took a toll on the bond we shared. Before we...

I shook that thought away.

Enzo and I were two people who agreed to marry for our own personal gain.

Falling for one another wasn't supposed to happen, but it was.

It was happening, and I could only hope that it was as real for him as it was for me.

"And I..." I pushed my hand into his dark slacks. "I've really missed feeling you inside of me."

I missed his hands and his mouth.

The way his chest rumbled when he moaned in my ear.

"Enzo..."

He lifted me, carrying my body through the kitchen and down a long hall where at the end, our bedroom sat. It was the only room in the penthouse that shared the same floor-length windows as the living room. He laid me on the California king-sized bed—the dark blue comforter molded softly against my skin.

"Let me help you balance it."

He came out of his shirt and slacks, giving me the perfect view of his toned chest and arms. The man was covered in tattoos. They were like a map of his thoughts and desires, a path only he could understand but somehow I did, too.

"You can't," I told him truthfully. "It's something I have to do on my own."

His eyebrows hiked.

"No?"

He was on me before I saw it coming, flipping me over onto my stomach and then pulling me up by wrapping his arms around my torso. My dress was up and over my ass now, exposing my little black thong, and then my entire body after he pulled it off altogether.

"I think I know a few ways to help you balance the stress, *Bellissima*," he whispered against the curve of my spine. "Tell me I'm lying, so I can prove otherwise."

I whimpered, completely seduced by his deep cadence. It was spellbinding.

"You aren't lying..."

How could I lie?

I knew—no matter how I answered—he'd give me everything I needed and wanted sexually. He had me on all fours, his hands cupping my breasts—fingers twisting my nipples—while kissing all over my back. My pussy thumped for him. She was so drenched that the silk fabric of my thong stuck to me. If that wasn't proof enough, I didn't know what else could be.

"Please," I moaned, submitting to him without a fight.

I backed firmly into his erection, practically begging the man to dick me down while he took his sweet time teasing me. He moved his pursuit up, sucking on the skin of my neck just below my ear before pulling the naked lob into his mouth.

Enzo freed up one hand and clamped his fingers around my throat, dragging me deeper into his chest. "Say it again," he ordered, his tone husky.

I could barely breathe, and it was exhilarating.

He loosened his hold but only enough for me to suck in two deep breaths before cutting off my supply again. "Say it, *Scarlatto*."

"Please, Enzo," I begged. "I want you."

He released me, pushing my body forward until my ass was arched in the air to his liking. Slowly, he dragged the thin material of my thong down my thighs and then off my body completely. There was a moment when the bed dipped, and the heat of his body disappeared, but it wasn't long before he returned, his face buried between my legs.

Oh, God.

He toyed with my clit from the back, sucking and slurping the nub as if there would be no tomorrow. I pushed down on his tongue, sliding my pussy down the length of it to maximize the pressure. *Goodness.*

I felt everything.

The slight tightening in my core.

The warmth of his saliva mixed with my essence.

"Mmm," I whimpered, gripping the duvet. "Eat this pussy just like that. *Sí!*"

Both of his hands came down on my ass, the slap so hard that I jeered forward. My pussy gushed from the impact, craving more—no, *needing* it. Enzo was too good with his tongue. Every lick and flick was strategic.

"Again," I cried out, my breathing labored.

I was so close.

He did it once more, striking me right over the last spot. The pain was almost blinding, but the feeling of pleasure that followed made it all worthwhile. He spread my cheeks, his fingers digging harshly into the supple flesh, and I sobbed. I wasn't able to control it or the orgasm that burst through me in waves upon waves.

Enzo gave me no time to recuperate. He had me by the neck again, my back arched against his chest as he slid into me with one swift stroke.

"You missed this?" he growled.

I could feel his smile against my ear—the confidence of

what he knew he did to me was evident. There was no denying that while my husband could eat pussy like no other, his dick game was top tier. *Crème de la crème*—the best of the best.

"Fuck me," I growled back.

He tortured me, starting his quest off agonizingly slow. The drawback and reinsertion drove me wild. Enough to lower inhibition and beg again. I needed more.

"P-Please!"

"God, I love when you beg me, *Bellissima*."

"Please, fuck me," I repeated for good measure, earning a long deep thrust that brought tears to my eyes.

Enzo flicked his tongue over a sensitive spot on my neck, sucking down as hard as he now fucked me. Our bodies pressed together, his fingers still cutting off some of my oxygen supply while he held me up by the torso. The man was fucking the shit out of me, and I let him with my mouth ajar and nothing coming out. It was so good it hurt.

"Let me hear you."

He slowed his strokes and loosened my neck by a small margin. A deep moan escaped me. I barely recognized my voice. *Shit*. I barely recognized myself when with him.

"What the fuck are you doing to me?"

I didn't care for the answer. I only wanted him to never stop.

"I'm fucking my wife the way she deserves after a long day of work."

He was relentless, wild, and unfucking civilized with the way he pounded inside of me. Fucking me like I was a bad girl who needed punishment. The rhythm of his strokes was perfect. He had one leg up, one knee into the mattress during a deep side stroke into my g-spot.

An orgasm so intense worked its way through my body, and

when I'd reached my peak, the ecstasy consumed me completely. I would never recover.

I fell into the mattress, my vision blurry and body spent but aware of Enzo still moving inside of me. His strokes slower, hands at either side of my face, while he found his own high.

"Fuck!" he moaned, almost in anger. "I'm losing my goddamn mind over you."

I smiled into the duvet, feeling smug about the way I made him feel. I arched up, and he snatched out of me, making me turn to catch his nut. He stilled, and cum shot out of him in long spurts, making a mess all over my mouth and chin. Enzo let out a low moan, and he stared down at me while I licked my lips clean.

"Don't move."

He got out of bed and went into the bathroom, returning with a warm washcloth. I let him clean my face, closing my eyes as he wiped my pussy next. I'd never felt more attracted to a man than him. The way he took care of me first, always.

"Come here," he said, pulling me into his arms after stretching out on the bed. He brushed his fingers through my hair and chuckled. "I fucked up this silk press."

"What do you know about silk presses?" I asked, yawning.

"I have a sister."

I smiled because having a sister wasn't the reason he knew; it was the fact that he *paid* attention to her. He knew things most men wouldn't understand because he took the time to. Maybe my dad was right. There wasn't a clear-cut definition of good or bad. Enzo might've been a criminal, same as me, but he had a good heart. And to me, what was on the inside mattered most.

I yawned again, trying my best to stay awake, but he'd worked my body into early hibernation.

"Sleep," he whispered into my forehead while gathering me closer.

"You'll be here when I wake up?"

"I'm with you for the night."

I heard him; my body believed him because before I knew it I was out. And when I awoke a few hours later, Enzo was spooning me. His knee pushed between my legs, arms wrapped around my body, and his breath on the back of my neck. I blinked through my haze, focusing my attention on the moonlit sky through the windows.

Ugh.

"Enzo," I whispered, reaching behind me to cup the back of his head. "I need to pee."

He released me but took the time to tweak my nipple and kiss my shoulder before doing so completely. I picked up my phone from the nightstand—noticing the few calls I'd missed from Gaia—and went into the bathroom.

"Oh, thank god," she rushed out the second the line connected us. "I thought we would have to reroute if you didn't call back soon."

I stared at myself in the mirror. My hair was a bird's nest, my eyes red, and body tired. What I wanted to do was climb back into bed with Enzo and let him hold me until the sun woke us up, but I couldn't.

"Are you here yet?"

"Almost... I'll see you in ten minutes."

She hung up, knowing there wasn't much we could say over the phone.

I quickly brushed my teeth and hair into a bun, washed my face, and then entered the walk-in closet from the bathroom. He'd had it split into *his and hers*. The space was big enough to be a studio apartment all in itself.

In less than five minutes, I was dressed in an all-black

sweatsuit and a pair of black Nikes. When I returned to the bedroom, Enzo was up from the bed and making his way over to me.

"She almost here?" he asked, leaning down to kiss my lips. He moved past me and began to get dressed.

"Yeah. Should be pulling in by the time we make it down there."

I hadn't expected him to be hands-on with the tunnel situation, but I also wasn't going to fight with him about being there. At the end of the day, he had every right to be. I watched him dress in dark clothing, the same as me, and then turn toward the shelf filled with shoes against the back wall. He slid his fingers over the bottom of a shelf, and it parted.

"I see someone has hiding places I don't know about."

"Now you do," he mused, pulling two KelTec P15 pistols from the large collection. "For you..."

I took what I now realized was a custom-made handgun. The polymer frame was black, while the barrel was a dark crimson-red color. My mouth watered at the beauty he'd just gifted me.

"This is..." I gripped the perfect-sized machinery. "It's perfect."

"These are registered. If you're in the building or over at the casino, always carry that one."

I nodded, tucking it on my person.

When I turned to leave the enclosed space, Enzo pulled me back, twisting me to face him again. His lips came down on mine, and I melted into him on contact. We stood there past the time we had needed to be gone and indulged in an intoxicating kiss.

Then he released me and said, "I told you about leaving me without a proper goodbye."

"We're going together," I pointed out, following him through the penthouse toward the elevator.

"And we don't know if we'll come back together."

The reality of what he meant, the truth in his words, urged me to kiss him once more.

He was right.

There was no guarantee we'd make it back to one another, whether we were together or apart. When you lived this life, anything could happen.

The elevator dinged, indicating we'd made it to the basement level. And as soon as the doors slid open, I heard my cousin's voice.

"I don't give a fuck what you're ordered to do. I'm telling you what's going to happen."

She and Brandon were standing face to face.

"No," Brandon said, shaking his head. "That's not how this is going to work."

I didn't know much about Enzo's cousin, but he seemed a little too uptight.

"What's the problem?" Enzo asked, stopping movement from everyone at work.

Enzo had a team breaking down shipments of guns that had come in less than twenty-four hours ago.

"She wants to take the ATV through," Brandon explained, his brows furrowed in irritation.

He had no clue what we were doing or why Enzo was allowing it. In fact, Enzo seemed to keep him in the dark about a lot.

"Give her the key," he ordered. "And you can take your leave."

I could tell he didn't appreciate what was being asked of him, but he did as he was told.

"He is a fucking prick," Gaia spit out. "It's three in the morning. What kind of casino manager is he anyway?"

"Mine," Enzo replied. "Be easy on my cousin, Gaia. He works best when rules are followed and while he may be a prick to you, he's an asset to me."

She huffed and spun around, key in one hand and tracking device in the other.

"Violet and Jaz are almost here."

We got into the ATV and made the mile trek to the other end, making it in two minutes flat.

Their tunnel was remarkable.

It was lit up with hanging lanterns, wide enough that the ATV could drive through it comfortably but still slightly narrow and rocky. When you reached the end, you take a ladder up above ground, and it led into a passageway under a bridge.

By the time we all made it out, the black transport van pulled in. I glanced at Enzo, wondering if he was really prepared for what he was about to see.

Gaia walked forward and opened one of the double doors, pulling it open slowly and ducking her head inside. You could hear their feet scrambling back, the whimpers.

"It's okay," she spoke softly. "You're safe."

Jaz and Violet hopped out and rounded the truck, both looking a little flustered.

"What's wrong?" I asked, rushing forward.

Violet looked away, turning to help Gaia.

"We couldn't get them all out, Luci," Jaz whispered. "Mekhi had to force Violet back into the van. I-I didn't know what else to do and—" she looked down for a brief moment, gathering herself. When her gaze met mine again, the pain was locked away. "There were way more than we could handle."

"Even with security lacking," Violet said, cutting her eyes at me. "It would have been too big a risk. We can't go back again."

Fuck. Fuck. Fuck.

That made me sad.

I should have gone, been there to get more out.

"Don't do that," Jaz said. "Beat yourself up. We can't save them all."

I took a deep breath and nodded, knowing she was right but wishing she wasn't.

"Where's Mekhi?"

Violet gave me a knowing look.

Mekhi Lewis had gone through *boarding* school with me. His background was sealed so tight, not even I could find anything on him, and I'd tried. But, in the end, not knowing his past didn't stop us from becoming friends. Whenever I couldn't physically be there with Jaz and Violet on a job, he took my place.

He never stayed too long, always willing to help but in the wind as soon as it was over. I had a feeling he did it for his own personal reasons, whatever they may be.

"What are we going to do?"

I walked over to the van, the doors were now wide open, and I got a look at the five girls inside—all minors. My insides twisted in anger. I wanted to massacre the entire Costa bloodline.

"Are any of you hurt?" I pressed my hands into my body for emphasis, in case they couldn't understand me.

"No," the oldest-looking one answered. "W-We were only roughed up a little bit."

She looked over my shoulder, her eyes widening in fear at the sight of Enzo looming behind us. He hadn't said a word, but I felt his presence.

"He's no harm," I said.

"That's..." she looked at me, a little more confident. "That's what they all say."

My heart felt that.

I understood all too well what she meant.

I turned to face Enzo, closing the distance between us in short strides.

"What do you do with them now?" he asked like he'd been waiting to get it out. "Where do they go?"

"There's a shelter in D.C. that helps women and children who've been trafficked find their families or start over. I think..." I glanced over my shoulder, feeling all eyes on me. "We usually keep them in one of the safehouses overnight and then make the drive."

His gaze pierced through mine.

"Keep them here. On the medical floor."

I opened my mouth, and he shook his head.

"For the night," he went on. "Let my staff look them over. I'll have Rocco come move the van wherever you want, and your girls can stay, too. Matteo is gone on business; I'll set them up at his place."

I could feel his mind working, checking off the calls he'd need to make.

"You handle getting them underground, and I'll handle the rest."

He grabbed his phone and turned, and I stood there like a statue, staring at his back in complete awe. The girls and I had never had this kind of help before, and a familiar emotion took root inside of me. If I had denied it before, there was no doing so now.

I was falling for Enzo Bianchi. *Hard.*

Chapter 18

Enzo

I knocked on the door to my father's office and pushed my way inside when he called for me to enter. "You wanted to see me?"

He waved me in further, and I took a seat.

My father being at the casino today alarmed me. He didn't frequent this location often after Matteo and I took over. When he was around, I was always privy prior to his arrival. His stomping grounds was the Myriad in Atlantic City—the more legitimate of the two.

I'd known when he'd asked to speak that the conversation wouldn't be one I liked. But I was itching to get out of here, handle my business, and then check on Lucia.

"When you came to me and proposed an alliance with the Moretti's through marriage, I knew there was more to it," he said, leaning back in the chair he occupied. "You two played a good game of strangers, but the minute you said *I do*, the shift was immediate."

"I didn't lie to you," I said, frowning. "You asked what the catch was, and I told you she was. Had I been wrong?"

She was the catch.

Her father's connections. *Her* connections.

Lucia had been the perfect person to pair with.

I couldn't help that our bond turned out to be deeper than I initially realized.

"I'm not calling you a liar," he clarified. "But I do want to know why I had to hear about what she's been up to from Brandon."

I clenched my jaw, a spark of anger slicing through me.

"Brandon doesn't know shit because I didn't tell him shit."

"Enlighten me then, son. Because from what I hear on the streets, he's not too far off on his assumptions. You do remember that I'm the head of this family, right? Your people answer to me before they ever answer to you."

"I'm well aware."

He rolled his chair forward and leaned into the desk.

"Enzo, what the fuck is going on in that head of yours that you thought it'd be okay to include yourself—and by extension—your brother and me in Lucia's attempt to overthrow a family?"

I chuckled.

"Is that what you think this is about? Her revenge story? To a family, she doesn't even fucking know?"

I couldn't explain how angry I felt.

My insides were boiling over. Not because he didn't understand but because he was questioning my judgment. When it came to business, I'd never given him a reason to believe that I didn't know what the fuck I was doing. Everything he instilled in me I took seriously—I took it to heart.

"I'm waiting for you to tell me."

"And I'm still waiting on what the end game is for the plan you convinced us to go along with. Letting Giovanni poke his nose in our business without consequence, allowing him…" I flexed my fingers. "...allowing him to disrespect my *wife*. All for what?"

Giovanni still had to pay for that, and he would.

My father appeared taken aback for a brief moment. I had never questioned him before, but on the flip side, he'd never questioned my moves either. Now we were at an impasse.

"The Costas put out the word that if their goods are returned by midnight tomorrow night, they won't retaliate. I'm ordering you to send the girls back, Enzo. I don't care how you do it; just get it done."

"What happened to the code you told me to follow no matter what?"

He shrugged, not moved by what I was asking.

"The code we live by is separate from that of the five families. The Costas are under the Commission's reign, and thanks to you, *we* fall under the Delegation. If the O'Sullivan, Sāto, Ivanov, or Moretti families ever cross that line, we can cross this bridge again. Until then, do as I say, *Figlio*."

"Is that final?" I asked, staring at the man who raised me in the eyes.

"That's final."

I nodded and raised up, my gaze still pinned on his.

He was daring me to defy him, and I almost hated to think about it, but that was exactly what I planned to do. Lucia had been right; this was bigger than us—the mafia. My father could turn a blind eye, but after I saw the look in those girls' eyes last night, I knew I couldn't.

"Understood."

I turned to the door but stopped—never turning around to face him—after he called my name.

"You have a good heart. But maybe that's what Lucia is playing at. Ask yourself this, why is she really doing this? I can guarantee it isn't what you think, but I'll leave you to figure that out with your *wife*.

Whatever he'd been trying to do, worked.

I knew from the moment I'd met her that there was more to the story. She never once elaborated, and I decided to wait for her to feel comfortable enough to do so. In order for me to defy the head of my family, and to take her side on this, Lucia had to come clean. *Today.*

I left my father's office and headed for the casino's security room. The exact place I knew Brandon would be. He was there as I expected, surrounded by a few guards, Malik and Rocco.

"Everybody except Brandon out!" I yelled, slamming the door shut to get their attention. "Now!"

The moment the room cleared of eyes and ears, I rushed my cousin, grabbing him around the neck and squeezing so tight he balked, eyes wide. My lips curled at the fear permeating from him.

"I know you think you run things around here," I sneered, slamming his back into the nearest wall as he fought to breathe. "But you must've forgotten that it was me who allowed you to have this small amount of power. Your job is to run the casino..." I lowered my head, my eyes drilling into his. "Not me, my fucking business, or my mothafucking wife."

I released him, and he slid to the floor, sucking in gulps of air and coughing.

"Stay in your place, Brandon. I'd hate to kill you. That would devastate my mother, and she's been through enough already."

"I did what I thought was best for the family," he wheezed out.

"What's best for the family isn't your business," I roared, my trigger finger itching. "It'd be best for you to remember that Lucia is a Bianchi now. Going against her *is* going against the family. Clean yourself up and get back to work." I paused at the door. "And the next time your aunt invites you to dinner, show the fuck up. What would your mother think?"

I walked out of the room to find everyone pretending to have not been listening.

"Fuck are y'all standing around for? Get back to work!" I glanced at Rocco and pointed. "You. With me." I cut my eyes at Malik. "Keep an eye on Brandon. If he even blinks in the wrong direction, you have my permission to shoot right past his ear and blow his eardrum."

Rocco and I moved in silence across the walkway.

He sensed my mood while I was trying to rein in the storm brewing inside of my chest.

"I need a favor, Roc..." we stepped into the elevators and hit the floor labeled M. "But first, I need to know that I can trust you."

He stared me directly into my eyes and said, "With your life..." he glanced up as the numbers ascended. "Lucia's too," he added. "I'm here because of you. My loyalty is with you and, by association, her."

I nodded, believing him.

We came to a stop, and the doors slid open to Matteo's apartment. My brother, who had clearly just gotten back from Atlantic City, stood in the living room where Violet and Jaz were still sleeping.

"Why are they here?" he asked, cutting his tired eyes at me over his shoulder. "With their feet on my couches?"

Rocco chuckled and swaggered in just as Gaia appeared—hair all over her head.

"Seriously," she screeched, rushing away.

"They had a long night..." I shrugged and moved toward the kitchen. "You weren't here."

Our apartments were identical in size and dark décor, but

that was where the similarities ended. Matteo had his place renovated, nixing the open floorplan concept I kept. It was only after I entered the kitchen that I spotted Lucia sitting at the table with a mug in her hands.

She stared straight ahead, her brows drawn together in worry.

"I fucked up," she said, glancing my way as I took a seat beside her. "My brother called. I can guess it's what your father wanted to talk about."

"More or less." I took the mug from her hands and set it aside. "What he had to say doesn't matter. I want to know what it is that you want to do."

The frown on her pretty face deepened.

"What I want to do? Enzo, you can't—"

"I can. I'm a grown-ass man with a mind of his own, and my gut is telling me that I need to rock with my wife. So, tell me, what do you want to do?"

For the first time in the nearly eleven months I'd known her, tears pricked the corners of her eyes. The sight of that made my chest tighten. I turned her chair to face me and slid it as close as I could.

"They were never going back," she said, not allowing the tears to fall. "I just… I thought I had it all together. And now, I don't know how to proceed."

"Sometimes not proceeding at all is the best plan of action," Matteo interjected as he entered the kitchen and opened the fridge. "Even when it'll kill you inside to put something that means a lot to you on the back burner, it's necessary."

Matteo leaned against the island with a bottle of water in hand. Rocco entered seconds later and hopped up on the counter, much to my brother's dismay.

She rotated in her chair.

"How many have you saved?" he asked.

"Five hundred and... *two*."

Rocco whistled.

"You did that with a team of four, including yourself."

"A team of two, sometimes three," she corrected. "Violet and Jaz didn't join until a couple of years ago."

It was something about the way she'd said it, the tone of her voice, that caught mine and Matteo's attention. He raised a brow in my direction, but I had nothing to give.

"Ah..." Rocco hopped down off the counter. "They're the... *and two*."

She nodded solemnly as Jaz, Violet, and Gaia entered.

"We need to—" Gaia paused, her eyes roaming the room. "Why are the four of you staring at us like that."

"I think they're staring at *us*..." Violet pointed to herself and Jaz. "And while it's quite uncomfortable, we need to go before it gets too late."

"I pray my couch was a comfortable reprieve for the night," Matteo mused.

"Mmhm," Violet hummed. "Even when I remember hearing a voice that sounded just like yours complaining about feet being on it."

Matteo grinned, lightening the mood.

"Before you go, we have to discuss something," Lucia said, standing up and walking toward them.

"Why do I get the feeling this isn't going to be good news?" Jaz asked.

"There are people on the lookout for your transport," I hopped in. "Pietro put word on the street. He doesn't know exactly who he's looking for, but nothing stays secret for long."

"So, then..." Violet's determined eyes met mine. "What are we doing?"

"Gaia and I will go—"

"No," I cut in, shaking my head at Lucia. "Fuck, no."

"You don't get a say," she snapped, angling her head at me.

I mirrored her stance, my arms crossed.

"That's where you're wrong. Do you know what they'll do to you if they catch you? What they'll do to Gaia?"

It was a low blow, using the love she had for her cousin against her, but I couldn't let her go. Not alone, without me. The drive to D.C. wasn't long, but so many things could go wrong in those three hours.

"I can handle myself."

"He isn't saying you can't," Rocco chimed in. "But logically, Enzo is right."

The girls stood facing us, ready to go to war about their operation. About the safety of those they'd saved, and if I weren't already in a fucked up mood, I'd find their solidarity cute.

"We don't need *his* permission," Jaz snapped, her dark eyes drilling into me. "I don't need it."

"No..." I shook my head. "*You* don't..." I looked at Lucia, who was daring me to say it with her eyes. "...but *you*, my sweet wife, need it."

If looks could kill, I'd be a dead man, and I would deserve it. But for the time being, I was standing on the move I'd just made.

"Matteo, help Jaz and Violet get the girls from the medical floor down to the basement," I ordered, my mind working on our next play while Lucia stood stock still, her anger evident. "Rocco, you and Gaia wait for them. Lucia and I need to have a little talk. No one leaves this fucking building without me knowing it."

"I don't know who—"

"Do it," Lucia cut in, turning to Gaia. "I'll be down in a minute."

With that settled, I walked past the group and grabbed Lucia's hand along the way.

"If you're going to kill him, try not to get blood on the floors," Matteo yelled. "It's a bitch to clean, and I want to be able to move in right away."

His attempt at a joke fell on deaf ears as the doors shut and Lucia flew at me. She hit me in my chest, and I let her, my eyebrows raised. The woman packed a punch, but I'd praise her later about it.

"You want to fight me, Scarlet?"

I walked past her and into my—*our* apartment.

"How dare you!" she shouted from behind me. "You don't run me, Enzo. I am a person who is free to make her own decisions."

I continued down the hall and into the bedroom, where I began to remove my hoodie while she ranted about her rights and some more shit I wasn't trying to hear.

"My God. You aren't even listening."

"I hear you loud and clear, Luci. Doesn't change that my decision is final."

"Final," she screeched in disbelief. "Who the fuck are you?"

"The man you agreed to marry," I said, removing my gun and watch and setting them on the dresser. "The man you let fuck you into submission every time I slide into you."

"Fuck you."

"I'd be glad to fuck that anger out of you, but we need to address a few things first." I turned to face her, and for a moment, I almost gave in. The look in her eyes hurt my fucking heart, but she wouldn't understand why it had to be this way until we really *talked*. "Go ahead..." I kept my arms at my side in the most non-threatening position I could muster up. "You want to take your anger out on me, do it."

She hesitated.

"What are you waiting for? You were ready to throw hands a few minutes ago. I'm giving you the opportunity. Your *only* one."

Her nostrils flared, her fingers balled into tight fists.

Lucia wanted to fight, but she couldn't bring herself to fight *me*.

That did wonders for my ego.

"I can't."

"Why not?" I asked, walking toward her. "Hm? You want me to fight you back? Put my hands on you?"

She held her ground longer than I expected before she started to back away. Eventually, I had her blocked in a corner where the wall met the window. The automatic blinds were down halfway, blanketing part of the room with darkness.

"Yes."

The answer had come out in a tiny whisper. All that bass in her voice disappeared suddenly, but the stubborn lift of her chin held strong. She didn't know how to fully submit to a man outside of the bedroom. I'd let Lucia do her thing, be herself. But when it came to her life, I wasn't sitting back and allowing her to walk into the lion's den.

"You know I can't give you that." I reached for her neck, and she slapped my hand away, the fire back. "Either take your chance or hear what I have to say."

I caught her split decision the second she made it.

Her knee swiftly came up, and I batted it away, ultimately missing the swing of her elbow next. She got me right in the chin, the short-lasting sting rushing through me and making my dick hard.

"Don't stop now," I taunted, stepping back to give her more room. "Keep going."

She came at me fast, her punch to my ribs just as quick.

I sucked in a deep breath and smirked, sending her into a blinding rage of coordinated moves that only made me want to fuck the shit out of her. Lucia swept her leg out, and I went down but not without bringing her with me.

We struggled on the floor until I got her in a position she wouldn't be able to get out of. I pinned her legs against mine by locking my ankles over hers and then sealed the rest of her in place with my arms.

"Let me go," she seethed, trying to writhe against me. "Enzo, I swear if you don't—"

I kissed her and rocked my pelvis into her core.

She lasted a good minute without reciprocating, but eventually, I got what I wanted. The low submissive moan rolled through her and directly into me. I loosened my hold and stared into her eyes, a realization hitting me.

I loved this woman.

And when she reared back and smashed her head into my nose, the feeling grew stronger. I'd managed to twist slightly, stopping her from breaking it but the pain from the impact I'd caught shot through me.

I was *in* love with her.

"Ah, fuck, Luci," I cursed, grabbing my nose and laughing. "That shit hurt."

"I'm glad you admitted something hurt," she quipped, straddling me—the warmth of her pussy sitting right on top of my stiff dick. "Let me see."

I let go, and she winced.

"Okay, it isn't broken."

I looked at the blood on my hands and then at her.

"Why is it so important to you?" I asked, not giving a fuck about my nose. "The truth. I can't have your back completely if I don't know everything."

She sighed, pressed her hands into my chest, and stared down at me.

"Because once upon a time, Lucia Moretti met a guy. She was too cocky. Fresh out of training, on her first job. Eyes wide..." she shook her head. "Maybe a little too wide. I fell for him. It hadn't developed into love, but it could have. I'm glad I hadn't allowed myself to do it. Because he turned out not to be who I thought."

She looked afraid to say, maybe even ashamed.

"You can trust me," I reassured, tone soft. "I won't judge you or make you feel less than the badass I know you to be. Whatever it is, I'm here to stay."

"He was a spotter for the Costas," she revealed. "A romancer, they called him. I'd become his target—his obsession—and it was all for his own sick and twisted pleasure. He'd known who I was, who my father was, and what we were to Pietro. I was a come-up, but he hadn't foreseen me being more dangerous than him. His story started to sound funny one day, and that's when I woke up. The haze cleared, and I figured it out with a little digging from Gaia."

Fuck.

I was angry for her.

"Does your dad know?"

She shook her head.

"I couldn't tell him. But I felt so bad, so stupid, for allowing him in my personal space that I plotted my revenge. Gaia and I followed him one night to a receiving dock near the Navesink River. He was alone at first, and then I heard the cries and whimpers, and something lit up inside of me. I lost it, and if Gaia hadn't been there, I don't know what I would've done."

I was piecing together all the telltale signs she's shown of being betrayed.

Not wanting to be touched.

Her dislike for made men.

The way she questioned my intentions with women, in general, every step of the way.

"You went back?"

"We saved only a few that day. Jaz came next. Violet, two years later. A host of others, all on our own."

"Is he still alive?"

"No, he isn't." Her lips curled into a menacingly sexy smile before it vanished altogether. "I do this—not because I'm righting a wrong or wanting to find the good parts of me in all the bad—but because there are women and young girls out there who don't have my training. *I* had my training and still almost got caught up. And to the very people who find my mere existence sickening."

I wrapped my arms around her waist and pulled her chest to mine.

"We'll put the girls on the jet to D.C.," I said, brushing my nose and lips against hers. I winced a little. "That's going to sting for a while."

"I'll make it up to you."

"Oh yeah?"

She slid down my body, purposely pressing her weight against my erection.

"Mmhm," she hummed, running her nose over the length of me through my joggers. "But first..." she jumped up, amusement dancing in her eyes. "We have to take care of our people."

I sat up and grabbed her hand before she got away.

She looked down at me curiously, and the words I'd been about to say evaporated.

"I've already lost enough people in this lifetime," I told her. "I'm not trying to lose you, too. Not when we're just getting started."

Not when I love you.

I pulled myself up and then her into my arms.

"You can't embarrass me like that in front of my people," she mumbled into my chest.

"And you can't make decisions that could affect your well-being without me."

Her life was mine to protect whether she liked it or not.

She was mine to protect.

And I would go toe to toe with her again and again until it was stamped into her mind that this was how it needed to be—how it *had* to be. For my peace of mind and my fucking heart.

Chapter 19

Lucia

I paced.

Enzo stayed with me as long as he could before he had to leave and take care of something with Matteo. The second he was gone, the worry set in.

Rocco had gone with Gaia to take the girls to D.C. by private jet. It had been the safest and quickest way to get them out of Jersey. They'd insisted I stay back.

Ugh.

Violet and Jaz wouldn't accept my invitation to stay and begged me to not follow them back to Blackthorne. I checked my watch and grabbed my phone, checking their locations and then calling.

"Luci," Violet answered. "I know you can see we're back at the condo. Safe and sound. Gaia and Rocco made it safe. Relax, mama."

I couldn't.

It all felt wrong.

"I don't know, Vi." I stood in front of the windows in the

living room, watching the sky change colors as the sun began to set. "I feel off."

"Because you aren't the one leading the pack right now," she said, sounding sure of herself. "I know you're used to being the person we lean on, but you have another life now. You have to let something go. I can't tell you what, but it has to be something."

We sat silently on the phone, and then she whispered, "Go figure that out, and we'll talk soon. I need a little break from trying to save the world."

The line went dead, and the corners of my eyes burned with tears.

I wasn't the crying type.

But twice in one day, they had formed.

"Unacceptable," I grumbled to myself, tossing my phone on the sofa and marching to the bedroom.

I walked into the closet and right to the built-in shoe shelf, running my fingers under the same shelf Enzo had. Because I'd fingerprinted my way into different parts of the building, I recognized the feel of the scanner. I pressed my thumb into it, and the shelf parted, revealing Enzo's stash.

Turning, I opened the top drawer splitting my side of the closet in half and pulled out my burner. I didn't need to accept another job from the Society for two more weeks. As long as I took no less than two jobs a month, I was in compliance. But I needed something to do, something to remind myself that I was still that bitch.

Two messages rolled in after it powered on.

I decoded them and scrolled to pick my new target.

The first one didn't appeal to me, but the next one...

I was caught off guard by the name.

Target: Brandon Santoro
Last known location: Grayfall, New Jersey

Pay: $5,000,000
Time frame: Forty-eight hours

The request had come in that morning, and the time frame to have the job done started the minute I accepted. I typed out my reply, my finger hovering over the send button, but for some reason, I couldn't bring myself to accept just yet. So, I tucked the gun Enzo made me promise to carry with me on the premises, shut the gun safe, and left the apartment with both of my phones on me. I went down three floors to the first medical suite, finding it empty. After checking the next, I went floor by floor, looking to see if Brandon was on this side of the walkway or on the casino side.

When I got to the main level, the doorman and security guard—who I recognized—greeted me.

"Mrs. Bianchi, do you need anything?" the doorman asked.

"I'm okay, Carlos..." I paused. "Actually, have you seen Mr. Santoro?"

"You just missed him," Orlando said, stepping away from his post. "He went back to the casino."

"Do you know why he was here?"

Orlando regarded me curiously but didn't push me for more.

"He was down in the basement for a short time, but I didn't ask him why. Something wrong?"

I shook my head and turned to take the elevator up to the walkway.

"Thanks, Orlando."

After twenty minutes of searching, I found Brandon in his office. He had the door wide open, so I slid inside, taking it as an invitation for anyone to enter.

"I'm sorry about my cousin," I said, startling him.

His head shot up, eyes wide until he realized it was me.

"Shit," he cursed, leaning back in his seat. "You're light on your feet."

I took a seat in front of his desk.

"You should be aware of your surroundings," I mused, picking up a photo of him and a lady that looked exactly like Emilia. "Your mother?"

He nodded, and I set it back in its rightful place.

"Do you miss her?"

"All the time..." he shifted his attention a few times, unable to look me directly in my eyes. "She was all I had after my father passed."

"I'm sorry you had to endure so much loss. I couldn't fathom."

I meant what I said, and his appreciative gaze met mine, telling me that my words meant something to him. The contract on his life didn't make sense. Sure, he was a little uptight, but I didn't sense someone who deserved to die.

"Do you know who I am?" He opened his mouth to speak, and I shook my head. "I mean outside of who my father is. Did Enzo tell you *what* I am?"

I sensed his confusion, which was the answer I needed.

"Growing up, I had this guard who I saw as my best friend. He taught me how to fight, how to hold a gun, take it apart, and shoot. It kind of became an obsession by the time I was twelve. Anyway, it turned out that my favorite guard had been assigned to me on purpose. When I turned seventeen, I learned the truth."

I wasn't sure why I was telling him this, but the words were pouring out of me, and I couldn't stop them even if I wanted to. Brandon's fear of where this was going got my blood pumping.

"What was the truth?"

"He was to groom me into a killer. I was to be molded into whatever the Red Society would need. Whatever the mafia would need. I felt betrayed because he was my family, you know? But I went anyway. I took on the challenge and excelled."

I stared at him, my gaze dancing over his face, looking for any sign of a traitor.

"Why..." he swallowed. "Why are you telling me this?"

I shrugged and sat back in my seat, placing my gun on my lap.

His eyes zeroed in on it, but he didn't make a move or openly react.

"Because ever since then, I take the betrayal of people who are supposed to be the most loyal to heart. By extension, that includes you, Brandon. I care for Enzo. Even when I'd initially come to him for something else, I knew he was one of the good ones. So, tell me..." I picked up the beautifully crafted KelTec. "Why am I here?"

"W-What do you mean?"

I angled my head.

"I think you and I both know what's happening here. But I need to know why you're on my radar. Who would ask me to do this to you?"

I narrowed my eyes at his small but significant hand movements.

Shaking my head, I sighed.

"You don't want to do that," I said, aiming the barrel of my gun at his head. "By the time you get your fingers on whatever is under your desk, the walls behind you will be painted with the insides of your head. Put your hands on the desk."

He obliged that shifty look in his eyes back.

"Are you in trouble? Made a decision you now regret? I need something to go on if this is going to work in your favor."

"I only did what I needed to for the family. There are consequences for every action. I'm prepared to accept my fate, but are you prepared for what will happen to Enzo because of yours?"

His question was like a slap to the face, but that unnerving feeling I'd had since Enzo left me worked its way back into my gut.

"I'm not envious," he said out of nowhere. "Betrayal in this world comes in many forms. Like what your longtime guard did to you. He's still on your bad side, I can tell."

"He never apologized."

"And is that all it takes? An apology? To make up for years of lies, manipulation, and hurt?"

"Who lied and manipulated you?" I asked, following the trail of breadcrumbs he seemed to be leaving.

"Not me."

He shook his head, eyes closed as if he remembered something important.

"My mother..." he rested his gaze on mine again, eyes tired. "She was always doing for others. Going out of her way to be a source of comfort to people who didn't deserve that part of her. It killed her."

The conviction in his tone—the sorrow.

It was real; this was real to him.

Whatever *it* was.

"You want revenge on those people."

It was becoming clear.

"Person. I want revenge on that one person. Turns out, he wants to take me out first." He cut his attention to the gun, his gaze following the length of my arm before adding, "How are you holding it steady for so long?"

I chuckled.

"Practice... *forced* practice."

"Sounds like torture."

"Made me who I am." I shrugged. "Who is it?"

"My father."

That gave me pause.

I even found myself lowering the gun slightly.

His father?

"I thought he was dead."

"The man who raised me is dead, but the one whose DNA I share is very much so alive, Lucia."

I ran down a list of names in my head. Checking them off, one by one, looking for similarities. Brandon was caramel complected. Lean, same as Enzo, but under six feet. Still taller than me but shorter than the Bianchi men. That didn't mean...

"Not him," he said, eyes knowing. "He loves my aunt and would never betray her trust by sleeping with her sister."

"But..." I lowered my arm completely, resting it in my lap. "Oh, Brandon. Why didn't you start with that when I walked in?"

"You're smart. I had a feeling you'd figure it out before putting a bullet in my head."

His lips lifted into a genuine smile.

"I like you," he went on. "For what it's worth... If you had killed me, I would've haunted Enzo, not you."

"It's good to know that you two are getting along," Enzo mused from the doorway, for once in the time I'd known him appearing without me sensing him. "That's the second time you've pulled a gun on my cousin, *Bellissima*."

He walked into the room entirely, his eyebrows raised and his nose slightly swollen. I winced, feeling a little bad for doing it to him.

"No hard feelings," Brandon said, winking. "She was only doing her best detective work."

"You could have told me off the bat," I reiterated, rolling my eyes.

Enzo flipped his snapback backward on his head, revealing

his nose more. The hat had been low on his face, enough to distract someone from noticing right away. Brandon glanced at me and then double back with wide eyes seconds later.

"The fuck happened to your nose?"

I tried not to laugh, but the sound burst out of me.

"I'm sorry," I said, rolling my lips in at the glare on Enzo's face. "I said I'd make it up to you."

And I had every intention of keeping that promise but first, the Brandon situation needed to be addressed.

"Does he know?"

"Do I know what?"

I stared at Brandon expectantly.

There was no way I would be revealing the truth—not when he was still alive to do it himself. Brandon looked afraid to say it, which told me Enzo had no clue.

What a fucking mess.

"Giovanni is my real father."

Enzo's stoic expression never changed.

I couldn't tell if maybe he'd known all along or if he was shocked. If he didn't care or find it noteworthy. There was no way of telling how it made him feel at all until he opened his mouth.

"Roberto—"

"Just raised me," Brandon clarified. "He'd known all along. I didn't find out until after my mom passed."

"Why didn't you say anything?"

"For what? Gio would never have me. I'm the bastard son who can barely hold his arm straight enough with a gun."

I smiled at his humor.

"Besides," he went on. "I'm with the family I'm supposed to be with."

I sat up straight, something about his tone of voice triggering a question that hadn't been answered.

"Why does he want you dead?"

"Ah..." he looked sheepish almost. "I confronted him to see if he knew. At first, he denied it, and then he admitted to knowing. He pretended to take an interest, but when the questions about *Zio* Angelo's moves started to come up more frequently, I realized he was using me."

"That doesn't answer why he wants you dead," Enzo pointed out. "What do you know that he doesn't want to get out?"

"I can't say."

"Why the fuck not?"

"Because I told your dad already, and he made me promise not to repeat it."

Enzo chuckled and swiped his thumb across his nose.

"Was it around the same time you told him about the transport?"

He shook his head, eyes dropping to the desk.

"Hey," I called, waiting until he lifted his head to continue. "Don't do that. Beat yourself up for wanting to know your father. For doing what you felt was best to protect the people you love when you realized he was up to no good. The same people..." I glared at Enzo. "...who love you back. Always keep your head up and stand on your decisions."

"She's good with words," he mused, looking over at Enzo.

"Yeah... that's how she caught me, too. With that mouth."

I rolled my eyes.

"I never told him about the transport. He already knew, and I couldn't lie once he asked."

Enzo nodded and held out his hand for mine, to which I gave with no problem. I tucked my gun on my person and looked up into his eyes.

"We'll figure it out together."

"Yeah..." he sighed, suddenly looking tired. "Later, though."

He pulled me to the door but stopped just short of walking out.

"I meant what I said about showing up to the family dinners," he said, confusing me, but it was clear Brandon understood after he nodded. "And I apologize for how I acted this morning. You didn't deserve that."

"It's all good, Enz." He waved him off. "If I were married to her, I would've reacted the same."

Enzo nodded and led me out, hand still in mine.

"What was that?" I asked when we made it onto the walkway.

"Nothing but me being man enough to admit when I'm wrong."

He cut his eyes at me.

"What's next?"

"Honestly..." he pulled me in front of him, and I wrapped my arms around his neck. "...I don't fucking know."

I nodded.

"Okay... let's not know together for a little while."

"A little while sounds good."

He backed me into the waiting elevator, his gaze still lingering on my face.

"You're beautiful, you know that?"

"I know."

He chuckled and the most genuine smile lifted the corners of his mouth.

"You're beautiful, too," I said, resting my head on his chest. "I never meant for you to take on my problems with yours."

Those words came tumbling out before I could stop them. And Enzo took his time responding, leading us into the penthouse and then the bedroom first. We fell into bed together, and he pulled me on top of him.

"I asked you to marry me, Luci," he whispered, softly kissing my neck. "I knew you were trouble."

"And you still wanted me."

"I *still* want you."

He caressed my back, fingers sliding over my skin in slow, soothing circles. I wanted to stay like this, with him, forever. He made me feel good inside. He made me feel *good* in general.

Goodness.

"Why do you believe in me so much?"

"Because you believed in me first, baby."

I pulled back and stared down at him.

"What do you mean?"

His lips slanted up on one side.

"You came to me because I had something you could utilize, yeah?"

I nodded.

"But do you remember exactly what you said to me?"

I thought back to that day in his bland office, but what happened was sort of a blur. What I did remember was him wrapping his fingers around my neck, me allowing him, and slicing his neck with the razor blade I had in my mouth.

I leaned to the left and glanced at his neck, noticing the faint scar.

"I remember doing that."

"*I heard you're a man of morals, Bianchi,*" he parroted, reminding me of exactly what I'd said that day. "You believed that enough to seek me out, to see for yourself."

"It was Monroe," I admitted. "She was vague about it, about you. But I figured it out."

"What else did you figure out?"

Resting my forehead against his, I kissed him slowly—living in this moment where we simply didn't know what was coming next but that we would take it on together when the time came.

His lips were meant to be against mine.

He was meant to be mine, and here we are, doing life together. Two people who might be a little off their rockers, finding something special with one another.

"That you *are* a man of morals," I mumbled into his mouth. "*My* man."

"Fuck, Scarlet..." he leaned back, my face in his hands. "I need to tell you something."

The tone of his voice, the look in his eyes...

"What is it?"

I hated the softness in mine—the hope I had that what he was about to say wouldn't break me. I wasn't sure I'd make it out of this one unscathed.

"Enzo..."

"I knew all along."

"You knew..."

I removed myself from his lap, needing space to think clearly.

"You knew what all along, Enzo?"

He sat at the edge of the bed.

"You..." he glanced at me. "I didn't know about that tattoo, but I knew you. *Of you.*"

I stared at my wrist, tracing the ink.

It was more than just a reminder of who I was, but a brand from the Society. They'd stamped us all. Even when I decided to leave, I would always be one of them.

"You aren't making any sense."

"Almost two years ago in New York at five-thirty in the evening, you were having dinner with Monroe at Blackstone Bar and Grill in Manhattan. You were wearing a long cardigan, that kind of looked like a dress. It was a mixture of tan, brown, and burgundy. Your hair was pulled into a low ponytail, and you had on red lipstick."

"I remember," I said, my stomach swirling. "She'd just had Storm."

"I saw you, and I couldn't think straight. I needed to know you, but Sheldon talked me out of approaching. Said you had a lot on your plate at that time but that if it were meant to be, I would find a way."

I glanced at him, seeing the sincerity in his pensive gaze.

"So, you found a way?"

"Monroe didn't just happen to mention me."

"It was all planned? Getting me to seek you out, so you could what? Convince me to marry you? Use me?"

He got up and walked around the bed to where I now sat, kneeling down in front of me.

"I didn't know you would come looking for help. I didn't know you would come at all. Monroe didn't exactly tell me she'd gone through with it; you showing up was a surprise, but I took it for what it was."

"Which was?"

"That we were meant to be."

A part of me felt duped by my longtime friend.

By Enzo for not telling me sooner.

The other part of me, the one that was already in love with this man, found what he was saying to be sweet. It made it more real for him and me, more human and less mafia.

"Asking you to marry happened on a whim. I should have told you after we got close."

"Yes..." I let go of my wrist. "You should have."

"But, I don't regret any of it. How we happened."

He maneuvered himself between my legs and pulled me into him, his face pressing into my stomach.

"I don't regret it either," I whispered, wrapping my arms around him and resting my chin atop his head. "None of it."

"Luci, I—"

"I know..." I shook my head, not ready to hear the words yet. "Me too."

Enzo lifted me from the bed, and I latched onto his waist with my legs. One minute we were kissing, and the next, he stilled, his head shooting up and brows furrowed.

"Do you hear that?"

The sound of the elevator was distinct.

A sort of whooshing noise and then a ding to indicate that it'd stopped on our floor. The silence that came after is what got us both moving, grabbing the guns we still had on us.

"No need for the guns, *Figlio*," Angelo called as we made our way slowly down the hall. "Though I think it's about time you secure this floor a little better now that you're married."

We found Angelo standing in front of the family portrait Enzo had up on the wall, his back to us.

"What's up, pop?"

"You and I need to have a talk about what's next."

Chapter 20

Enzo

"I haven't been completely honest with you," my father said, turning to face Lucia and me. "About the reason why we left the family and branched out on our own."

He hadn't needed to be honest.

I was there.

I watched Giovanni and other high-ranking members of the family force his hand and push us out. There wasn't anything more than that. It is as simple as black and fucking white.

"What more could there be?" I asked, annoyed that now he wanted to include me in his *full* plans. "You were pushed out. *We* were."

He shook his head.

"I'm afraid that isn't quite true..." he cut his dark gaze over to Lucia, who looked as confused as I felt. "You, Ms. Moretti—"

"Bianchi," she corrected, proving that she was in this with me.

My father chuckled and nodded.

"When he'd come to me about marriage, I thought it was

because he felt obligated to bring more to the table. Then, I met you, and I understood why my son would be so enamored with you, Lucia. Why he would suddenly throw away his disdain for arranged marriages and propose one himself. He saw in you what most seem to when they encounter you."

"What's that?" Lucia asked.

"An equal. Someone just as fierce and swift and forward-thinking. A woman who deserves to have it all while never asking for it. He saw a Queen. I don't know if you've noticed, but when men see you, they stare. Your aura is bright. Some fear what you're capable of, while others see your potential."

"And you? What do you see?"

"The woman who my son defied a direct order for."

"Because it wasn't the right one," I cut in. "You know it, too. So, why'd you give it?"

"If you had listened, then you wouldn't be ready to take my place. A leader hears what his people are saying but how he responds is what matters. The decision you made was for the best. Your grandfather would have been proud."

His words startled me.

"The same grandfather who left no direction for his family. He died, and they turned on you."

"No..." he shook his head. "He died with everything laid out. I was to take over; Giovanni was to be my second. You were to follow."

The same way I'd felt when we disconnected ourselves from the only people I knew and trusted was how I felt at this very moment. Betrayed. Tossed aside. Forced into seclusion.

"I know it doesn't make sense to you right now, but it will when you really process what I'm saying to you. Your mother and I did everything to shield you and your siblings from the lingering stares. The whispers about not being *pure*. I couldn't help the family I was adopted into, but I had all the power to make sure that my Black sons and daughter were able to stand on their own. I gave you the tools, removed you from the environment that enabled you, and look at what you accomplished."

"You lied," I said, my chest tightening with anger. "The one thing you promised you'd never do, you did it. Why didn't you tell us the truth? I would have... *we* would have followed you regardless."

Everything that had been happening started to make sense.

Giovanni fucking with our gun shipments.

Drugs in the casino.

My staff kept secrets while others betrayed my trust.

"It was you this entire time?"

"I only exposed who's loyal to you and who isn't."

"Fuck!" I shouted, tapping the wall beside me with my gun. I hadn't realized I was still holding it. "This was some kind of sick and twisted test? Is that what the fuck you're saying?"

"Enzo..."

"No, there's nothing sick and twisted about it. You stand better on your own than you ever would have had we stayed with Giovanni. Enzo, you are meant to have your own family. The one you built on your own from the ground up. Have you noticed the alliances you've formed? The people you know who will come running if things go left? Your *Zio* would have exploited you. I saw a way out, and I made the move."

"Why did he agree?" Lucia asked, stepping closer to me. "To let you all go if he saw Enzo's potential? Wouldn't he try all he could to stop it?"

He stared at her with an easy smile on his face that got my blood boiling.

"We had an agreement," he revealed. "One year. If we were to fail on our own, then I would return as his second."

"And then he met me..."

He nodded, the smile growing.

"And then he met you, and this trial run took on a life of its own. He should've never touched you. None of that was a part of the plan, but you sort of ruined his."

"I'm known for doing that sometimes."

He chuckled and then looked at me, that fatherly expression I was used to, crossing his face.

"How does Brandon come into play?" I asked.

"He learned the truth after becoming suspicious of Giovanni. I led him to believe that it was his sperm donor's attempt to sabotage and that kept Brandon at bay. He's loyal to you."

"Did you know Giovanni was his father?"

"It was news to me."

"I'm having a hard time with this," I admitted. "Right now, I need to sit on it."

He gave an understanding chin lift.

"I need to go have a conversation with your brother." His gaze shifted between Lucia and me. "When you're done sitting on it, we can discuss you moving into my place. This operation is yours, Enzo. It was always meant to belong to you and you alone."

My father left me with that, once again changing up my entire life without my permission. Taking away my right to choose my own path. It burned me up inside, but deep down, I felt the weight lifting. Or shifting.

"Baby—"

I grabbed Lucia and pushed her up against the wall, sealing my fingers around her neck and brushing the side of her face with the other. She was a sure thing, this woman. The person I could depend on to have my back but also see reason when I simply couldn't.

"What do you want out of this?" I asked.

"I don't..." she licked her lips, drawing my attention to them. "I'm not sure I understand what you're asking me."

"I'm asking you if this life is what you want. If being the Queen to my King in the Bianchi Crime Family is what you truly want."

She'd been fighting, unknowingly, for a place in this world for a long time. But I wondered if this was what she truly desired. If the life that I knew I was born to lead was our future or not.

"I could be wrong, but I'm getting that feeling that you'll leave this all behind for me."

His eyebrows were hiked high in disbelief. As if choosing her seemed absurd, but if she thought otherwise, then she truly had no idea the impact she had on me. How the love I felt for her was more important, and without my Queen, this life would be colorless. Pointless. Dull.

"I would leave this all behind for you," I confirmed. "In a heartbeat."

She took a deep breath and leaned into my fingers.

"Enzo, I would never let you give this up..." she grazed the length of my nose with the tip of her index finger. "...but to know that you would? And for *me?*" she shook her head. "I want to do life with you. No matter what that entails, as long as we are together, I'll follow you."

That confirmation was all I'd needed.

Relief filled me, and I smashed my lips into hers, telling Lucia exactly how I felt about what she'd just said through action. She wrapped her arms around me and moaned into my mouth. The sound vibrated through my chest and settled there, taking root.

She pushed me suddenly, backing me into the wall behind

us, pushing us farther down the hall. Lucia smirked and stepped forward and slid down in front of me.

"I promised I would make up for headbutting you."

She pulled at my joggers, focused on me.

"Mmm," I hummed, letting my head fall back against the wall as she released and stroked me to life. "Show me how sorry you are."

"With pleasure."

She slowly worked my length into her mouth, pressing her tongue to the underside of my dick simultaneously. Then she devoured me whole, widening her mouth and taking more.

Fuck.

Her mouth was wet and warm, her throat tightening around the head.

"Just like that, *Bellissima*." I wrapped my fingers around her bun and tugged, forcing her closer to me. "Fuckkkk."

Through low lids, I watched her suck and jerk me off with both hands at rapid speed, never taking her eyes off me. It was the sexiest shit I'd ever seen. And it felt better.

Cupping the back of her head, I thrust forward.

"Mmm," she hummed, nodding for me to do it again.

I kept stroking the inside of her mouth, tapping the back of her throat and holding it until she slurped up the saliva dripping from her lips and around my shaft.

"Shit... Scarlet, I—"

My attempt to pull out of her mouth was stopped by Lucia hollowing her cheeks and driving her forehead into my abdomen to keep me inside. I came so hard I was damn near seeing stars.

"Goddamn, Luci..." I pulled her up and into me before claiming her lips with mine. "Fuck were you trying to do to me?"

"Make you forgive me."

I chuckled and rested my forehead against hers.

"I want to do life with you, too," I told her.

I had my Queen and an empire I hadn't expected to be mine this soon. Shit was falling into place as my father—unbeknownst to me—had planned. No matter how I felt about the way he'd gone about it, I was up for the task.

Chapter 21

Lucia

"I thought I heard you two out here..." I pushed my damp curls out of my face and eyed the closeness of Rocco and Gaia. "Portia called and said everything went smooth."

Rocco moved around the island and opened the cabinet, filled with my coffee mugs. He pulled one out that had *Talk less, more coffee* scrawled in a dark blue color, and walked over to the electric kettle. I watched him and then cut my eyes at Gaia, who also had her gaze on his easy movements.

I cleared my throat, and her head snapped in my direction, eyes smoldering.

"What?" she asked, blinking away the lust.

"Portia said everything went smooth with the drop-off," I repeated.

"Oh, yeah..." another slow blink. "We were in and out."

Rocco chuckled and turned, placing the mug in front of her.

"Drink."

"Did *something* happen?" I asked, lips curling.

They'd left two days ago and stayed in D.C. on a whim. I hadn't questioned Gaia when she said they wanted to make sure they were being careful. But I'd also been preoccupied with Enzo. *Distracted.*

"Nothing happened," she said, rolling her eyes.

I lifted an eyebrow at Rocco.

"If I ordered you to tell me, would you?"

He smiled wide, showing off the dimple I'd somehow missed in his left cheek and rows of pretty white teeth. As unhinged as the man was, he was undoubtedly handsome.

"No can do," he replied, shaking his head. "When I make promises, I keep them."

He tossed me a knowing look, and I nodded.

"Touché."

Gaia watched us, narrowing her eyes at me and then him.

"You two have a secret?"

"Do you *two* have one?"

She picked up the coffee mug and sipped.

"Thought so..."

The elevator dinged, and I glanced over my shoulder, already knowing it was Matteo and Enzo making their way back from the basement. Enzo walked up behind me and buried his face into my neck, sniffing.

"Lavender," he whispered against my ear.

I nodded, though it hadn't been a question.

He straightened but kept his arms around me, pulling me deeper into him.

"Everything went good in D.C.?" he asked, making Gaia choke and Rocco smile.

"Everything was everything," Rocco mused vaguely.

Matteo, who'd had his head in our fridge, closed it and asked, "Fuck does that even mean?"

"A question I'd love an answer to..." I smirked at Gaia, and she threw up a middle finger before standing. "Don't leave, G. I'm only joking."

"I know. It isn't that. I need to check on the safe house and then go see my mom. She's been calling nonstop."

I nodded and removed myself from Enzo's hold.

"I'll walk you down."

We got onto the elevator, and the second the doors closed, I turned to her.

"Gaia..."

She shook her head, eyes closed.

"He's fucking insane!" she yelled. "Out of his fucking mind. Off his rocker. And so damn beautiful."

She opened her eyes, and there was this dreamy look dancing in them.

"He knows he's good-looking too," she went on. "It drove me insane being near him."

The elevator doors opened to the parking garage, and I looped my arm through hers as we exited. We walked silently to her car and leaned up against the trunk, facing the row of dark Escalades and sedans.

"You deserve happiness."

She chuckled.

"It won't be with him. This life..." she sighed. "It takes a toll. I need a little peace, you know? For a little while."

I understood how it could feel that way for her.

She'd only come into this with me, *for* me.

Because I had been spiraling after my ex, ready to slaughter any made man who looked guilty of sex trafficking or treating women badly in general. It took a lot of looking from within for me to come out of that.

"I appreciate you for everything. Without you, I don't know what I would've done."

"We are family before any of this. I'll always have your

back. If you ever have to kill Enzo and get rid of his body, I got you."

I chuckled and laid my head on her shoulder.

"Matteo has dibs on the penthouse if I do that, so I'm certain he'll assist."

She laid her head against mine, and we stood in silence for a while. I had so much on my mind, so many things I needed to say but felt like I couldn't. The pressure I'd put on my girls while away and leaving them to deal with a lot on their own was unforgivable.

"I realize that I can't do all of this and be fully present with Enzo."

"Have you been talking to Violet?"

"She might be the person I heard it from, but I've known before he ever came into my life that I was taking on more than I can handle. Enzo just... he makes me want to be all in with him."

I knew I wouldn't leave the Society until Storm was old enough to take my place. That was a long time from now but ample opportunity for me to guide her in the way I could only have hoped Joaquin had done.

"Then be all in, Luci," she whispered, draping her arm over me. "It won't make you no less of a badass. Violet and Jaz are ready to take the reins. I'll be around for them as I know you will, too, if need be."

I nodded.

"I need to handle something first, but after that, I'll try my best to step back."

"You don't have to do it..."

She lifted her head and stared into my eyes with those beautiful light brown eyes of hers, the concern evident. But this wasn't that. It wasn't a revenge plot, and it hadn't been for a while now.

"I do, but I promise I won't do it alone."

"You and Enzo are a real thing, huh?"

I sighed, feeling that dreamy look I'd seen in hers during our elevator ride wash over me.

"I'm in love with him."

"It's nice to hear you admit that."

I cut my eyes at her.

"Are you saying you've known all along?"

She laughed and pushed off the trunk, popping the locks with her key fob.

"No comment..." she pulled open the driver's side door and slipped inside. "I'll text you when I make it back to Blackthorne. Be good. No bloodshed."

"I know how to be a civilized human being."

She burst into laughter.

"You and your wombmate are both full of shit, but I love you both dearly. Later, girly."

I shook my head, my lips curved upward as I grabbed one of the scanners from the wall and checked her car just in case. After nodding that she was good to go, Gaia shut her door and drove out of the parking garage.

The elevator doors opened as I approached them, and Rocco stepped out.

"Glad I caught you," he said, handing me a folded-up piece of paper. "Your move."

He swaggered off without another word, and I tucked the intel away.

It was most definitely my move.

The last one to be made.

Chapter 22

Enzo

"What are you going to do?" Matteo asked as we sat outside of our parents' brownstone.

I cut my eyes at him.

"You're my consigliere; what do *you* think I should do?"

He smirked, and I saw more of our mother in him at that moment. We shared similarities, but he looked more like our father than I did. I was Emilia through and through.

"I trust your judgment. You've never steered me wrong."

"When you and dad talked—"

"I don't know how to feel about what he did..." he sighed. "I understand seeing bigger for your children, but to keep us in the dark wasn't cool. Nonna knew all along."

I shook my head and opened my door, prompting Matteo to do the same.

We hadn't seen our grandmother in almost a year.

No contact of any kind.

To take his test so far that he removed us from the one person who had always fairly shown us love fucked with my head. All this time, I'd been blaming her for not really caring, and it hadn't been true.

Shaking my head, I followed Matteo in, and we headed straight for our father's study. He had the door open, and his head lowered, eyes focused on something in front of him.

"Your grandfather's will," he said, acknowledging our presence without looking up. "He left a large chunk of money for the two of you and your sister."

The old man barely tolerated us.

At least, that had been how it felt.

"We don't need his money," Matteo said, sitting.

I kept my place at the door, leaning one shoulder into the frame.

"No..." our father finally looked up. "We've made a pretty on our own. I'm leaving you two to figure out what you'd like to do with it."

"Is that what you wanted to meet with us about?"

He met my gaze with a contemplative one.

"You're still angry?"

Was that a real fucking question?

It'd only been a few days since he dropped the news of his actual plans on me.

"I'm not asking," he clarified as if he were reading my mind. "I know you well enough to know that it won't be easy getting back into your graces."

"Then why didn't you tell me to avoid this? Huh?"

I kept as cool as I could, but deep down, I wanted to disrespect the man I respected more than anyone on this godforsaken planet. He was the one person I looked to for guidance and the same man who led me astray for almost eleven months. Maybe I was being irrational, not thinking logically but with my heart instead.

"I've been standing at your side since I could walk," I went on, deciding to get the shit off my chest and be done with it. "Wanting to be like you, make you proud. Every decision you've ever made, I followed without second-guessing it because I trusted you."

"And I needed you to be able to make decisions without seeking my approval, *Figlio*."

"Yeah, well, you hurt me in the process."

He nodded in understanding.

"I accept what came from the process. What I need to know is if you accept the outcome?"

"And if I choose not to?"

He almost looked amused by my retort, like he'd seen it coming.

"We both know you won't do that. Not when this is what you've been bred to do. You're angry, but you aren't stupid..." he glanced at Matteo, who'd been sitting quietly with his back to me. "Neither of you are. In fact, the two of you together is what Gio fears."

As if on cue, the deep baritone of the very man we were now speaking of carried through the brownstone.

Matteo stood and backed himself into the wall to my left while I stayed blocking the door, my gaze on my father. His lips curled at the corner, but he did not let the smile grow.

"As an apology," he said, his voice just loud enough for only Matteo and me to hear. "You cannot kill him, but he is alone."

"It is impolite to block doorways from others entering, *Nipote*."

The smug lilt in his voice, as if he were untouchable, was enough for me to react.

I spun around, grateful he was close enough to grab the back of his neck and drive his head into the wall. He let out a muffled yelp, and I repeated the move, bringing my knee up and into his gut at the same time.

"Being impolite is my new specialty," I spit out, letting him fall.

"You're asking to die."

He rolled over onto his side, his hand covering his nose in an attempt to stop the bleeding. I kneeled over him, snatching the gun he had tucked on his person and shoving it into his mouth. His eyes widened. Seeing him envision death brought a smile to mine.

"Dying is the only thing this life guarantees. Don't find yourself there sooner than it's your time, *Zio*. My wife is off-limits. If I even dream of you thinking of her, I'll kill you. No one, not even my father, will be able to stop me. You're smart. Don't sway from what you know in an attempt to best me either."

I released him and then bashed the side of his face with the butt of his own gun, knocking him out cold. It wasn't enough, but it would do.

I turned and handed the gun to Matteo, straightening my clothing right after.

"Do you feel better?" my father asked, his frame looming behind Matteo's.

"No," I admitted. "I'd rather have killed him."

"Do you accept?"

I cut my eyes at him, taking a moment to respond but ultimately giving him the answer he'd known I would provide.

"I accept."

He nodded.

"You two go. I'll take care of my brother and make sure he understands the consequences he'll bare if he retaliates."

I left without another word, one place on my mind.

One person.

When I made it home, I stepped off the elevator to the smell of herbs and spices.

My stomach growled, and I looked around, searching for Lucia but not finding her near the front. I took the short walk to our bedroom and knew exactly where she was. After removing my clothes and leaving them in a pile on the floor, I entered the steamy enclosed space.

"Welcome home, baby," she murmured from under the spray after I slid back the shower door and stepped inside.

"How'd you know it was me?"

I grabbed her by the waist and pulled her back into my chest.

"Because I can sense when you're near..." she tilted her head back to see me, those brown eyes I'd fallen in love with darker than usual. She took my hand and slid it up her stomach, letting it rest right over her heart. "I feel you here." She pushed my other hand down, between her thighs, and I parted her lips. "And... T-There," she whimpered as I rubbed her clit slowly.

"You cooked."

Lucia hummed while rolling her hips.

"For you."

I slipped one finger into her wet pussy and then another.

"Why?"

"Because from this day forward, you'll have the luxury of homecooked meals whenever you please. Not only on scheduled days."

My dick hardened, and I pressed it into her ass, shifting a little to add tension.

She'd heard me, tucked the information, and acted without needing guidance. It hadn't been about the meal itself but the sense of family that came with it. I loved mine, but something about starting my own with Lucia made everything I had to go through to get here worthwhile.

I pressed the palm of my hand into her clit, while vigorously fucking her with my fingers. She whimpered my name over and over, begging me to make her cum—to make her feel good. I sank my teeth into the fleshy part of her shoulder and pinched her nipple until she jerked, her body convulsing in my arms.

"I love you, *Bellissima*," I whispered into her ear, still stroking her through the orgasm.

Our gazes met, and she graced me with the most gorgeous, sated smile I'd ever seen.

"*Ti amo, Signor* Bianchi," she moaned, eyes falling shut and then open again. "*Tanto—so much.*"

Chapter 23

Lucia

While Enzo dressed, I grabbed the piece of paper that Rocco had given me less than twenty-four hours ago. I hadn't been completely forthcoming about why I wanted Pietro—my absentee grandfather dead.

In the beginning, it had been about seeking revenge for the lies my ex had told, for the way he tried to drag me into a world he had no clue I was already so connected to. But, it turned out that his coming into my life brought someone else in as well. And when I learned that my father and grandmother hadn't been the only ones wronged within the Costa of ranks, I decided to team up with a Costa himself.

"What's that?" Enzo asked, walking out of the closet bare chest and a pair of basketball shorts on.

I unfolded it, stared at the contents, and then handed it over.

He took it, his curious eyes on me, before looking at what Rocco had written down. I sat in the middle of the bed with my eyes pinned on him, wondering how he would feel about not knowing beforehand.

"I'm not following..." he sat down on the edge of the bed in turn to me. "I mean, I know what this is. I know where it is. But why do you need to know?"

I grabbed my body oil from the nightstand, poured some in my hand, and then spread it all over his back. For a moment, we just sat in silence, and then I decided to just get it the fuck over with.

"The truth is that I'd shot Pietro Junior at his request."

I waited with bated breath for him to say something, anything, but that never came.

"He sought me out," I went on. "He wanted to get to know me. I was reluctant, but something about him made me sit and listen, and I'm glad that I did. He had no clue that my father even existed until he returned to the East Coast. And when the whispers started about Pietro's long-lost son, his namesake decided to do some digging."

Enzo let out a deep breath, and I found myself doing the same.

"So what you're telling me is you and your *uncle* are conspiring against his father, your grandfather."

I wiped the excess oil off my hands and got out of bed so that I was standing in front of him. The same move he pulled with me when revealing that he'd known me all along, I mirrored. I kneeled in front of him and looked up into his eyes.

Those beautiful cinnamon browns.

"The only reason why I didn't tell you was that I needed to be sure that he wasn't setting me up..." I brought his fingers to my lips and kissed them. "I had him under surveillance for a little while, and it turned out that he was on my side. He was the one who lessened security at the docks. He was the one who gave us Mariana. He pulled through, and now I have to hold up my end of the bargain."

"And that is?"

"I have to kill his father."

Enzo started shaking his head before I could even finish the statement.

I knew he wouldn't like it because, as a member of the Red Society, I could not kill a made man without the permission of the Society and/or the Delegation or Commission. And Pietro Senior was not just any made man; he was a boss. Killing him could ruin me, but also, I knew that I could do it without anyone ever knowing that it was me. I needed Enzo to believe that so we could officially move on.

"Luci.." he tucked his hand under my chin while still shaking his head at me. "I knew you were fucking trouble."

I got up and climbed into his lap, wrapping my arms around his neck. With my forehead pressed to his, the tips of our noses together, and our mouths mere inches apart, I smiled.

"I know that this is a big deal, but I also know that is the right thing to do."

"Before I can let you see this through, I need you to promise me that this is it."

I pulled back slightly, my brows furrowed, praying that he wasn't asking me to promise what I thought he was. There was no way.

"You wouldn't dare—"

"You are absolutely right," he cut in. "I would never ask you to give that up."

"Then what are you asking?"

"I'm asking you to promise me that this will be the last time you put your life on the line when it comes to the Society, Commission, or Delegation..." he gripped my chin and pulled me forward. "I can't run our family and worry about you."

"I can take care of—"

"I know what you can do. In fact, I find that shit sexy, but I need you moving smart when we're apart."

For some reason, I couldn't stop the smile that stretched across my face.

"And how do you need me to move when we're together?"

He lifted me up and tossed me onto the bed and climbed between my legs seconds later. Enzo kissed my neck, down my chest, and cupped my breasts with both hands. The man took his time sucking on my nipples until I was a writhing mess.

"I need your crown on, head up, eyes fierce, and when problems arise, I want you to point, and I'll shoot."

He knew exactly what talking like that would do to me. I loved when he spoke violence, but in that soft cadence he used when only speaking to me. This man was everything. He was my *everything*.

"Say it again," I moaned, rubbing his erection through his shorts.

"When you're with me, all I need you to do is point, and I'll shoot."

"No questions asked?"

Enzo came out of his shorts moments later, pushing my legs further apart and thrusting into me. *Hard and fast.* I cried out at the way his thickness filled me, the way he wasted no time fucking me into capitulation. There was no holding back, and I loved every minute of it.

"No *fucking* questions asked," he moaned low and deep into my ear while stroking my pussy so good it hurt. "Not for you, *never* for you."

I came so hard that my vision blurred, and my body became rigid.

"Breathe, baby," he coached, stroking my neck with his thumb. "That's right. One more time."

I sucked in a deep breath, released it, and immediately, my body relaxed.

"Good girl." He kissed my lips. "Better?"

I nodded and rolled us over, maneuvering his body behind mine and cuddling me close.

"So, when are we going to kill Senior?"

I laughed; it came out loud and boisterous because I knew there was no way he was gonna let me go alone. But I was okay with that.

"He's there every week on the same day your mom hosts family dinner. We have to wait a little while but I'm patient."

He hummed and squeezed my body as if he were trying to drag me closer. I couldn't, but if there was an option to live in his skin, I would.

"It's a date."

I let my eyes drift close, sleep slowly taking me under.

"*Ti amo*," I whispered.

"*Ti amo, Bellissima.*"

Epilogue

Enzo

Four Months Later

"Baby..." Lucia's soft voice filtered through the earpiece I was wearing.

I sat in the back of a sedan with Malik at the wheel while we idled two blocks away from *Menage*. The sex club had been a famous rumor when I was a kid. But I learned how real it was as an adult, the things that transpired in it, and where it originated. Even those tiny details hadn't prepared me for what Lucia had to share about *Menage*.

"I'm here," I said, resting my head against the seat. "It's almost time."

I could hear her moving, trying to find a place that wouldn't fuck up her shot from on top of the building. The wind whipped through the earpiece, a tale-tell sign that fall had arrived.

"I wanted to tell you something," she said, sounding

nervous. "And at first, I wanted to do it face to face, but now I'm getting antsy."

I sat up a little bit, looking at Malik through the rearview mirror and glancing out the window. She'd made me promise to let her do what she'd agreed to without interfering. I would have preferred to be the one pulling the trigger. But, I also trusted her judgment.

"It can't wait? I'm going to see you in less than five minutes."

She chuckled softly, and I smiled.

"It's just that... For the last couple of weeks, these words have been in my head, and I can't get them out. Now I'm getting the urge to sing it to you right now, but I can't do it face to face because I'm shy."

Shy?

It was my turn to laugh.

"Aren't you the same woman who said calling you shy was offensive? When did that change?"

"That was before you made me feel butterflies," she murmured. "No one has ever made me feel like that before."

"Glad to be the first, *Bellissima*."

She released a breath that sounded more like a moan.

"One second..."

I listened closely, not able to hear anything but aware of what was happening—what she was doing. Malik started to cruise down the first block, knowing what was needed from him without being prompted.

"I'm back," she said, helping me to breathe again.

I never understood when I heard the women married to men in the mafia talk about how nerve-wracking it was to see the person they love leave, not knowing if they would ever come back. And it wasn't until I met and began to live my life with someone involved in the same shit as me that I got it. Every time we separated, my heart would beat irregularly, and it wouldn't return to its natural rhythm until I placed my eyes on Lucia at the end of every night.

"I need to know—"

"You have my entire heart," she began, cutting me off. "When I said I wanted to do life with you, I knew exactly what I meant at that moment. I hadn't thought about all the other things that come with doing life with someone you love. I just knew I would follow you wherever you went because this life doesn't make sense without you. I've been living in the moment with you, and every second of every minute, of every hour, of every day that passes, I find myself falling more and more in love with you."

I'd already felt complete with her, where our lives had gone in the last four months. Those words filled me to capacity and fed my soul.

"I—"

"And now," she continued, her frame coming into view as we reached the second block. "Now, I get to not only share this life with you, but *we* created a life that will share parts of us."

I didn't see myself as an extremely emotional man, but I wasn't ashamed to admit that I had real feelings. And for a moment, I felt my eyes sting at the revelation she had just dropped on me.

"Are you telling me that I'm gonna be a father?"

Malik rolled to a stop, and she climbed inside just as he began to drive away, the door swinging shut behind her. I snatched the earpiece out as she climbed into my lap, her hands going straight for my face.

"I'm telling you that now we get to do life with a little reminder of the love we share."

She pressed her lips into mine, and we shared a slow and sensual kiss, her body melted into mine. Every emotion I was feeling, I tried to convey with my mouth. But there was only so much physical contact that could help express what I needed to say, what I needed her to hear.

"I knew you and I would be special together," I told her, our lips just barely touching. "I found in you what I'd unknowingly been searching for longer than I can fathom. This..." I pressed my hand against her flat stomach. "...a family I know will be here with me, doing life, until we can't anymore. If I had to do it all over again, I'd choose you. Without pause, without any doubt, and in a fucking heartbeat."

She rested her head on my chest, and we stayed that way the entire drive to Blackthorne for dinner with her family *and* mine. It was the first of many, and I could already envision what it would look like in the years to come when the next generation of Bianchi's and Moretti's made their entrance.

"Ti amo, Bellissima."

"Ti voglio bene anch'io." I love you, too.

It took one sinful vow to get us here, and I would do it all over again.

As long as it was with her. *Only her.*

The End

Author Notes

Thank you for reading.
I hope you enjoyed the first book in the Mafia Misfits series.
Next up... Luca Moretti.
Please leave me a review on Amazon and/or Goodreads.
Interested in viewing a Pinterest board with visuals from the book?
Link: https://pin.it/5LSCuss
Here are a few ways to stay connected with me:
Website: www.asiamonique.com
Like me on Facebook: http://bit.ly/AuthorAsiaMonique
Join my readers' group on
Facebook: http://bit.ly/ForTheLoveOfAsiaMonique
Follow me on TikTok: https://vm.tiktok.com/TTPdkpVDvK/
Follow me on Instagram: www.instagram.com/__ayemonique

Printed in Great Britain
by Amazon